FYODOR DOSTOYEVSKY was born in Moscow on October 30, 1821. He was educated in Moscow and at the School of Military Engineers in St. Petersburg, where he spent four years. In 1844 he resigned his Commission in the army to devote himself to literature. In 1846, he wrote his first novel, *Poor Folk;* it was an immediate critical and popular success. This was followed by short stories and a novel, *The Double.* While at work on *Netochka Nezvanova,* the twenty-seven-year-old author was arrested for belonging to a young socialist group. He was tried and condemned to death, but at the last moment his sentence was commuted to prison in Siberia. He spent four years in the penal settlement at Omsk; then he was released on the condition that he serve in the army. While in the army he fell in love with and married Marie Isaeva. In 1859 he was granted full amnesty and allowed to return to St. Petersburg. In the next few years he wrote his first full-length novels: *The Friend of the Family* (1859) and *The Insulted and the Injured* (1862). *Notes from Underground* (1864) was in many ways his most influential work of this period, containing the wellsprings of his mature philosophy: the hope of gaining salvation through degradation and suffering. At the end of this literary period, his wife died. Plagued by epilepsy, faced with financial ruin, he worked at superhuman speed to produce *The Gambler,* dictating the novel to eighteen-year-old Anna Grigorievna Snitkina. The manuscript was delivered to his publisher in time. During the next fourteen years, Dostoyevsky wrote his greatest works: *Crime and Punishment, The Idiot, The Possessed,* and *The Brothers Karamazov.* The latter book was published a year before his death on January 28, 1881.

Fyodor Dostoyevsky

The
Possessed

TRANSLATED BY
ANDREW R. MacANDREW

WITH AN AFTERWORD BY
MARC SLONIM

(Revised and Updated Bibliography)

A SIGNET CLASSIC
NEW AMERICAN LIBRARY

NEW YORK AND SCARBOROUGH, ONTARIO

SIGNET, SIGNET CLASSIC, MENTOR, PLUME, MERIDIAN AND NAL
Books are published in the United States by
New American Library,
1633 Broadway, New York, New York 10019,
in Canada by The New American Library of Canada Limited,
81 Mack Avenue, Scarborough, Ontario M1L 1M8

12   13   14   15   16   17   18   19   20

PRINTED IN CANADA

Contents

PART ONE

Chapter 1	By Way of an Introduction: Some Biographical Data on the Worthy Stepan Trofimovich Verkhovensky	9
Chapter 2	Prince Hal—Matchmaking	41
Chapter 3	Another's Sins	78
Chapter 4	The Cripple	120
Chapter 5	The Wise Serpent	152

PART TWO

Chapter 1	Night	197
Chapter 2	Night (Continued)	243
Chapter 3	The Duel	267
Chapter 4	General Anticipation	279
Chapter 5	Preparing for the Gala	301
Chapter 6	Peter Verkhovensky Gets Busy	326
Chapter 7	Among Friends	369
Chapter 8	The Fairy-Tale Prince	394
Chapter 9	At Tikhon's (Stavrogin's Confession)	405
Chapter 10	A Search at Stepan Verkhovensky's	443
Chapter 11	Freebooters—A Fatal Morning	453

PART THREE

Chapter 1	The Festivities Begin	478
Chapter 2	The End of the Festivities	508

Chapter 3   The End of a Romance   539
Chapter 4   The Final Decision   560
Chapter 5   A Lady Traveler   584
Chapter 6   An Eventful Night   615
Chapter 7   Stepan Verkhovensky's Last Trip 647
Chapter 8   Epilogue   681

Afterword by Marc Slonim   695
Selected Bibliography   702

Can't be helped, the track is covered.
Hopeless! We have lost our way.
Demons must have taken over,
Whirling, twisting us astray.

. . . . .

Look at them! They're everywhere!
Hear the mournful tune they make!
What, a witch's wedding fare?
Or a goblin's gloomy wake?

> *(from "The Demons,"*
> *by Alexander Pushkin)*

And there was there a herd of many swine feeding on the mountain: and they besought him that he would suffer them to enter into them. And he suffered them.

Then went the devils out of the man, and entered into the swine: and the herd ran violently down a steep place into the lake and were choked.

When they that fed them saw what was done, they fled, and went and told it in the city and in the country.

Then they went out to see what was done; and came to Jesus, and found the man, out of whom the devils were departed, sitting at the feet of Jesus, clothed, and in his right mind: and they were afraid.

(Luke 8:32-37)

Part One

chapter 1

BY WAY OF AN INTRODUCTION: SOME BIOGRAPHICAL
DATA ON THE WORTHY STEPAN TROFIMOVICH VERKHOVENSKY

I

In approaching the recent, very strange events that occurred
in our hitherto rather unremarkable town, I feel that I must
start further back by supplying some facts about the life of
the gifted and well-respected Stepan Trofimovich Verkhovensky. This may serve as an introduction to the story to come.

Let me begin by saying that Stepan Verkhovensky had
always cut a rather special figure among us—in the civic sense,
that is. He passionately loved his role—so much so, in fact, that
I don't think he could have lived without it. But don't think that
I mean to compare him with an actor—God forbid—I respect
him too much for that. It may have been largely a matter of
habit, or rather a constant and even praiseworthy tendency,
ever since his childhood, to slip into a pleasant daydream about
his taking a gallant civic stand. Thus, he greatly relished his
idea of himself as a *persecuted* man—in fact, an *exile*. There is
about these two words a certain traditional glamour that se-
duced him once and for all. As the years went by, by exalting
this glamour he placed himself, in his own estimation, on a
pedestal that greatly gratified his vanity.

In an eighteenth-century English satire, Gulliver, returning
from the land of the Lilliputians, where the people were only a
few inches tall, had become so used to thinking of himself as
a giant that, back in London, he kept shouting at the carriages

and people in the street to get out of his way so that he wouldn't crush them. They laughed at him and insulted him, and rude coachmen even lashed at him with their whips. But were they justified? What may not be done through habit? And it was habit that made Stepan Verkhovensky act as he did—and, after all, his behavior was milder and less offensive, for he was really a very nice man.

Although in the end he was completely forgotten, I think it should be said that he had had a certain reputation. There's no doubt that at one point—a very brief moment, to be sure—his name was mentioned almost in the same breath as those of Chaadayev, Belinsky, Granovsky, and Herzen. But Stepan Verkhovensky's active engagement ended almost as soon as it began, because of what he described as "a whirl of events." In fact, though, it turned out that there never had been any "whirl" or even any "events" to speak of. Only recently I learned for certain that Mr. Verkhovensky's reason for living in our province was not that he had been exiled from Petersburg and Moscow; nor was he ever under police surveillance as we had been led to believe. Such, then, is the power of autosuggestion! Throughout his life, he himself sincerely believed that in certain government quarters they were very apprehensive of him, that his every step was watched, and that each of the three successive governors we had during twenty years had, on assuming his post, been warned about him by very highly placed, powerful people and consequently was full of misgivings on taking over the province. And if one of us had ever tried to persuade Mr. Verkhovensky that he really had nothing to fear, he'd certainly have taken it as an insult. Yet, at the same time, he was such an intelligent, gifted man, and his learning . . . well, it's true that there were no special academic achievements to his credit; in fact no achievements at all, I believe—but then, this is so often the case with our learned men in Russia.

When he returned from abroad in the late eighteen forties, he shone briefly as a university lecturer. Actually, he only had time to deliver a few lectures—on Arab culture, I believe. He also managed to defend a brilliant dissertation on the social and Hanseatic influence the little German town of Hanau might have had between 1413 and 1428 had it not been for certain special, rather cloudy circumstances. That dissertation was a clever, telling dig at the Slavophiles of the time and made him many enemies among them. Later, after he lost his position at the university, he succeeded in having published (just to show them whom they'd lost!) in some progressive monthly that often carried translations from Dickens and advocated the theories of George Sand, the beginning of some very profound study of, I believe, the underlying reasons for the extraordinarily high moral standards of some knights or other during a particular historical period, or something of that sort. In any case, he developed in it some subtle ideas of unbelievably high moral caliber. It was rumored later that continuation of the study had been forbidden by the authorities and even that the progressive magazine had suffered unpleasant consequences for having carried the first part. Well, it's very possible—all sorts of things happened at that time. In this particular case, however, it is more probable that nothing like that happened, that the author was simply too lazy to complete his research.

As to his lectures on Arab culture, they had to be discontinued because, at one point, someone—probably one of his reactionary enemies—wrote a letter to someone else informing him of certain matters. Whereupon someone asked him for certain explanations.

I can't vouch for it, but I have heard that at that time they discovered in Petersburg a monstrous, subversive organization of about thirteen members that had come close to blowing the regime sky-high. It was said that they were about to start translating Fourier himself! As chance would have it, the Moscow authorities just then seized a verse play that Stepan Verkhovensky had written six years earlier in Berlin, when he was still very young. The manuscript was being circulated from hand to hand and had already been read by two poetry lovers and one student.

That manuscript is lying on my desk in front of me now. I received it about a year ago from the author himself, who had only shortly before that recopied it in his own hand. It bears his signature and is bound in sumptuous red morocco.

I must say there's a lyrical quality about the play; perhaps it even shows some signs of talent. It's a little strange, but that's the way they wrote in the eighteen thirties. It would be difficult to tell you what it's all about, for to tell the truth, I can't make out a thing. It's some sort of allegory in lyrical-dramatic form that somehow reminds one of the second part of *Faust*. The action opens with a female chorus followed by a male chorus. Then there's a chorus of "occult" forces, and finally a chorus of human souls who haven't lived yet but would like

to have a go at it. All these choruses sing something very obscure, mostly about a curse laid on someone or other. However,
they handle the subject with delicate humor.

Suddenly the scene shifts and something called the Festival
of Life takes place. Now everyone sings, including the insects.
A tortoise arrives and says a few sacramental words in Latin.
And, if I remember correctly, even a mineral (an inanimate
object beyond all doubt) bursts into song at one point. In general, the lot of them hardly ever stop singing; when they do
talk, it is only to exchange some vague invective—and even in
this there's a hint of profound significance.

Then the scene shifts again. It's a wild, rocky spot, and
among the rocks a civilized young man is out for a stroll. He
keeps picking herbs and sucking them. When a fairy inquires
why he is sucking them, he informs her that he feels an excess
of life within him, that he's trying to forget himself and find
forgetfulness in the juices of these herbs. But, he tells the fairy,
his main wish is to rid himself of his brains—a wish that sounds
quite superfluous. At this point, an incredibly handsome youth
rides in on a black steed, followed by a huge crowd of people
of all nationalities. The youth is Death, and all the people are
thirsting for it.

Finally, in the closing scene, the Tower of Babel crops up.
Some athletic-looking men are helping to complete its construction while singing a song of new hope. When they have com-
pleted the job the lord of something (Olympus, I believe) flees
ignominiously, looking ridiculous, and mankind, having gained
insight into things, takes over and immediately starts to live
differently.

Anyway, this was the play that they thought dangerous. Last
year I suggested to Mr. Verkhovensky that he have it published, for it is quite innocuous by our present standards. He
spurned my suggestion with obvious displeasure. He didn't at
all relish my calling his piece innocuous, and I think this accounts for his subsequent coolness toward me that lasted for
two months.

And what do you think happened? At the very time I suggested that he have his play published here in Russia, it was
printed abroad in a revolutionary anthology without his knowledge. Terribly scared, he scurried over to see the governor and
wrote a noble letter of self-justification to Petersburg. He read
it aloud to me twice, but never sent it off because he didn't
know to whom to address it. He worried about it for a whole

month. I'm certain, however, that in the secret recesses of his heart he was immensely flattered. He went to bed every night with a copy of the anthology that had been smuggled in to him, and during the day he kept it under his mattress. He didn't even allow the maid to make his bed during all that time. And, although he daily expected to receive a telegram from somewhere, he maintained a haughty, resolute expression. No telegram arrived. Eventually he forgave me too, which shows how kind he is and how unable to bear a grudge.

II

Of course, I'm not trying to say that he didn't suffer for his convictions at all. But I'm convinced that he could have gone on lecturing about his Arabs if he had only provided the necessary explanations. Instead, he let himself be carried away by his imagination and convinced himself that his academic career was shattered by a "whirl of events."

But, if you wish to know the real truth, the actual cause of the break in his career was a renewed offer, made in the most delicate terms by Varvara Petrovna Stavrogin, the wife of Lieutenant General Stavrogin and an extremely wealthy lady. She suggested he take upon himself, in the capacity of educational supervisor and friend, the education and intellectual development of her only son, for which she offered him, it goes without saying, fabulous remuneration. The offer had first been made when he was still in Berlin, after his first wife died. She was a native of our province, a frivolous girl whom he had married while still very young and impulsive. I believe he had a miserable time with that (it must be said) rather charming woman, partly because of financial restrictions and partly because of certain difficulties of a delicate nature.

She died in Paris, having been separated from him during the last three years of her life, leaving him a five-year-old son, "the fruit of our first, still unclouded happiness," as Mr. Verkhovensky once sadly put it in my presence.

The fruit of their happiness was immediately packed off to Russia and his education entrusted to some distant relative residing in a remote backwater.

That first time, Mr. Verkhovensky declined Mrs. Stavrogin's offer. Less than a year after his wife's death, for no particular reason he married an uncommunicative Berlin girl. However, this remarriage was not his only reason for declining the position as young Stavrogin's tutor: he was fascinated by the resounding fame of a certain professor and had his eye on an academic career for himself that he fancied would give him an opportunity to soar on eagle's wings.

So, with his wings already singed, he recalled the offer that even before had made him hesitate. Then the sudden death of his second wife less than a year after they were married decided him definitely. Let me say candidly: it was all made possible by Mrs. Stavrogin's warm understanding and classical friendship—if that adjective may be applied to friendship. He threw himself into the arms of that friendship and nestled there for twenty years. Now, although I say he "threw himself into the arms of . . ." let no one start imagining things: those arms must be understood in a highly moral sense. The most subtle, delicate link united these two remarkable people once and for all.

Stepan Verkhovensky also accepted the tutorship because the small estate he had inherited from his first wife was close to Skvoreshniki, the Stavrogins' magnificent estate near our town. Moreover, Mr. Verkhovensky felt that, in the quiet atmosphere of his study, undistracted by the immensity of the university load, he could devote himself to learned research and to enriching the treasure house of our national culture. No results of research actually materialized; what did materialize was the possibility of becoming, for the rest of his life—for over twenty years—the essence of reproach to his native land. As the poet put it:

> The essence of reproach you stand
> To your beloved native land,
> You liberal idealist.

Of course, the person the poet had in mind may perhaps have been entitled to stand in a reproachful pose for the rest of his life, boring though that might be. But Stepan Verkhovensky really only imitated such people, and besides, as standing took too much out of him, he often curled up on his side for a little rest. Still, he managed to remain the essence of reproach even in a recumbent position, and that was good enough for our province. You should have seen him when he sat down to a card table in our club. His whole person seemed to say:

"Ah, cards . . . Imagine me sitting down to play cards with you! I know it's most unsuitable. But whose fault is it? Who shattered my career? Ah, what is Russia coming to?"

And with an air of the utmost dignity, he'd play a heart.

As a matter of fact, he was very fond of cards, which fondness, especially later on, caused frequent and unpleasant squabbles with Mrs. Stavrogin, particularly since he constantly lost. But more of that later. In the meantime, let me only say that he was a highly sensitive man (in some ways, that is) and so was often depressed. During their twenty-year friendship, he had periods of what we called "social grief" two, three, or four times a year. Actually, they were simple fits of depression, but Mrs. Stavrogin liked to ascribe them to his suffering over social injustice. Later, in addition to his periods of "social grief," he slipped into periods of champagne drinking. But, with great tact, Mrs. Stavrogin tried to help him control this vulgar inclination. Yes, he needed a nurse of sorts, for he grew quite strange as time went by. Now and then, in the middle of a period of the most noble grief, he suddenly burst into laughter that was anything but refined. Occasionally, he even made humorous remarks about himself, and there was nothing Mrs. Stavrogin feared as much as a sense of humor. She was a woman classicist, a lady-protector-of-the-arts who acted only out of the loftiest considerations. The twenty-year influence of this lady upon her poor friend was decisive, so a few words about her personality may be pertinent.

III

There are strange friendships in which the two parties long to tear each other to pieces most of the time and yet cannot live without each other. Separation is unthinkable because the one who loses his temper and decides to break it up would probably die himself if he went through with it. I know for sure that on several occasions, after an intimate conflagration with Mrs. Stavrogin, Mr. Verkhovensky suddenly leaped up from the sofa where he was sitting and banged on the wall with his fists. And I don't mean that figuratively either. Once he even knocked down a good deal of plaster.

You may wonder how I can possibly know such an intimate detail. Well—suppose I witnessed it myself? Suppose Stepan

Verkhovensky himself often sobbed on my shoulder, painting his secret torments in the most lurid colors? And the things he told me on some occasions!

But, the day after sobbing like that, he was prepared to crucify himself for his ingratitude. He would hurry over to my place or summon me hastily just to tell me that Mrs. Stavrogin was an angel, the soul of tact and noble behavior, while he was just the opposite. And he not only confided in me, he often described everything to her in the most eloquent letters in which—above his full signature—he confessed, for instance, that only yesterday he had told an outsider that she kept him out of vanity, that she was envious of his talent, that she hated him and only concealed her hatred because she was afraid he would walk out on her and thereby compromise her literary reputation; that, finally, he loathed himself and had decided to die by his own hand and was only waiting for the word from her that would seal his fate—and so on. So you can imagine the pitch of hysteria this innocent, fifty-year-old babe could work himself up to! Once I read one of those letters; it was written after a quarrel between them that had started over some trivial matter and had become envenomed as it dragged on. I was horrified and begged him not to send it.

"Impossible . . . it's more honest this way . . . my duty . . . I'll die if I don't make a clean breast of everything—yes, everything!" he muttered as if delirious, and sent the letter.

And this is where the main difference between them lay—Mrs. Stavrogin never would have sent a letter like that. True, Mr. Verkhovensky was crazy about writing. He wrote to Mrs. Stavrogin even though they lived in the same house, and during his hysterical periods, he turned out two letters a day. I know for certain that she always read those letters very carefully, even when she received two on the same day. Then she folded them neatly, annotated and classified them, and filed them in a special drawer. Moreover, she did some soul searching over those messages herself.

But then, having left her friend wondering for the whole day, she met him and behaved as if nothing had happened. Gradually she trained him so well that he never raised the subject of a quarrel himself, but only glanced questioningly into her eyes. However, she never forgot anything, whereas he did—and too quickly at that. Often, on the very next day, encouraged by her polite composure, he laughed in the presence of strangers and even behaved with schoolboyish exuberance over the champagne. I can imagine the venomous looks she darted at him without his ever noticing. But then—perhaps a week, a month, or even six months later—he would recall by chance some expression from one of his letters and then the entire letter with all the circumstances that surrounded it, and he would suddenly be overwhelmed by shame. This tormented him so that he always ended by suffering violent stomach upsets. He usually suffered from these upsets after periods of nervous strain; they were a curious feature of his physical make-up.

Indeed, Mrs. Stavrogin must often have hated him. But he had become, above all, a sort of son for her—a creation, her own invention. And this Mr. Verkhovensky never suspected to the end of his life. Yes, he became the flesh of her flesh, and she held on to him, but not at all because she was envious of his talent, as he asserted. Ah, how insulting such assumptions must have seemed to her! She buried her unquenchable feeling for him under constant hatred, jealousy, and scorn. She protected him from every speck of dust, looked after him like a baby for twenty-two years, and spent sleepless nights when she sensed some threat to his reputation as poet, scholar, and fighter for social justice. She had invented him, and she was also the first to believe in her own invention. He was a bit like a part of her private daydream. Consequently, she made great demands upon him, almost making a slave of him.

Besides, she was incredibly unforgiving. Let me tell you a couple of anecdotes about that.

IV

Once, when rumors about emancipation of the serfs first started circulating and all Russia was rejoicing in anticipation of a moral regeneration, Mrs. Stavrogin received a visit from a baron from Petersburg, a man with the highest connections and very closely associated with the forthcoming reform. She valued such visits highly because, since the death of her husband, her links with high society had become weaker, destined, as they were, to break altogether in the end. The baron came to tea, staying for about an hour. She didn't invite anyone except Mr. Verkhovensky, who, she felt, would be a good showpiece for the baron. Apparently the baron had heard of him—unless he just pretended he had—but, anyway, he scarcely addressed him during tea. Of course, Stepan Ver-

khovensky felt he had to make a good impression, which should
have been easy with his elegant manners. For, although he was,
I believe, of humble origin, he had been brought up from
earliest boyhood in a well-known Moscow family and spoke
French like a native Parisian. He was present to help the baron
realize from the first glance the sort of people with whom Mrs.
Stavrogin surrounded herself even in her provincial isolation.
However, it didn't quite pan out that way. When the baron
confirmed the absolute authenticity of the rumors about the
great reform, Mr. Verkhovensky allowed his enthusiasm to
get the better of him, shouted "Hurrah!" and even gestured
with his hand, intending to emphasize his exaltation. His
exclamation wasn't loud and was quite elegant in a way. His
outburst may even have been deliberate and the gesture carefully rehearsed before a mirror half an hour before the tea
party. Still, something must have gone wrong, because the
baron indulged in a very slight smile—although immediately
afterward, with incredible politeness, he managed to slip in a
phrase about the nation-wide delight, the lifting of all Russian
hearts at news of the great event. Soon after this, he left, not
forgetting to thrust two fingers into Mr. Verkhovensky's hand
in parting. When they were back in the sitting room by themselves, Mrs. Stavrogin remained silent for three minutes, osten-
sibly trying to locate something on the table. Then she suddenly
looked directly at Mr. Verkhovensky. She was very pale and
her eyes flashed as she hissed at him:

"I'll never forgive you for this!"

The next day she behaved as if nothing had happened, and
the incident seemed forgotten. Thirteen years later, however,
she suddenly recalled it during one of their quarrels and reproached him for it. And she turned pale and her eyes flashed
just as when she had reproached him thirteen years earlier.

Only twice during their entire relationship did she say to
him, "I'll never forgive you for this!" The tea party with the
baron was the second time. But the first time was also typical
and so affected Mr. Verkhovensky's life that I believe it should
also be told.

It happened in May 1855, when the news of General Stavrogin's death reached Skvoreshniki. That frivolous old man
died of a stomach upset on the way to the Crimea, where he
was to have joined units engaged in military operations. Mrs.
Stavrogin, a widow now, went into full mourning. It must be
said, however, that she cannot really have been very hard hit

by her husband's death, for as a result of the complete incompatibility of their characters, they had been separated for over four years. She paid him a monthly allowance, for the general had only a hundred and fifty serfs, his army pay, a well-known name, and good connections, while she owned the Skvoreshniki estate and was the only daughter of a very rich contractor. Nevertheless, the suddenness of the news was a shock to her, and she retired into seclusion. It goes without saying that Mr. Verkhovensky remained constantly at her side.

May was in full swing. The long evenings were enchanting; the wild cherry was in flower. Every evening they met in the garden and sat till nightfall in the arbor, pouring out their thoughts and feelings. Those were very poetic moments. The change in her marital status somehow made Mrs. Stavrogin very talkative, and, one might say, she opened the recesses of her soul to her friend. This went on throughout several May evenings.

Then a strange thought suddenly occurred to Stepan Verkhovensky.

"Maybe," he wondered, "this inconsolable widow expects me to propose to her when the year of mourning is over?"

There's no doubt that this was a rather cynical thought, but then, the higher the stage of development a man reaches, the more prone he becomes to cynicism, if only because of the increasing complexity of his make-up.

He mulled over this thought for a while and came to the conclusion that it looked very much like it.

"Yes," he mused, "there's a huge fortune here, but . . ."

Indeed, Varvara Stavrogin could hardly be described as a beauty. She was tall and bony, and her complexion was yellow. Her face was immensely long, reminding one of a horse. Mr. Verkhovensky suffered growing misgivings and hesitations that even reduced him to tears once or twice (in general, he had a propensity for tears). Now, during their evening meetings in the garden, a faintly whimsical, sarcastic expression crept over his face; his bearing somehow became both smug and coy at the same time. These things happen to one involuntarily, and the more noble the person, the more it shows. It is hard to say, but possibly nothing to justify Stepan Verkhovensky's suspicions ever stirred in Varvara Stavrogin's heart. In any case, she would hardly be likely to wish to exchange the name Stavrogin for Verkhovensky, glorious though he may have made it. Perhaps it was simply a feminine play on her part, a display of unconscious female needs common to women under certain circumstances. I can't say for certain: to this day, woman's heart has never been explored to its depths.

Undoubtedly, it didn't take her long to decipher the queer expression on her friend's face, for she was as sensitive and observant as he was innocent. However, their evenings didn't change, and their conversations remained as exalted and lofty as before. Then, once, as night fell, they said good night, warmly pressing each other's hands at the door of the annex in the middle of the garden, into which Mr. Verkhovensky moved every summer from the huge Skvoreshniki house.

He had only just gone inside, and full of disturbing thoughts, he picked up a cigar. Before lighting it, he stopped wearily in front of an open window, looking distractedly at the light, cottony clouds gliding past the neat crescent moon. A sudden crackle made him start and turn. Varvara Stavrogin, whom he had left four minutes before, stood before him again. Her yellow face had turned almost blue; her lips were pressed tightly together and their corners quivered. For ten silent seconds her hard, merciless stare transfixed him; then she spat out in a quick whisper:

"I'll never forgive you for this!"

Ten years later, when Mr. Verkhovensky related this sad story to me in a subdued whisper behind locked doors, he swore that he had been so petrified that he neither saw nor heard Mrs. Stavrogin leave. And, since she never so much as hinted at what had happened and their relations continued just as before, he was inclined to think it had been a hallucination such as precedes illness, especially since he actually was ill for two weeks, thus, by chance, putting an end to their evening meetings in the garden.

But despite his hope that it had only been a hallucination, he kept expecting what may be termed an outcome to the affair. He couldn't believe that it had ended then and there. And so, at times, he must have felt strange looking at his lady friend.

V

She even decided what clothes he should wear to the end of his days. It was elegant and appropriate attire: a long black frock coat buttoned almost to the top and very well fitted; a soft, wide-brimmed felt hat (a straw one in summer); a white cravat with a full bow and loose ends; and a cane with a silver knob. She also made him wear his hair long and flowing onto his shoulders. His hair was dirty blond and had only recently started to go gray. He was clean-shaven.

It was said that in his youth Stepan Verkhovensky had been very handsome, and in my opinion, he was extremely impressive even in his older years. But then, is fifty-three really old? Yet, in his desire to pose as an old fighter for social justice, he certainly didn't try to look younger than his age. He even seemed to want to emphasize his advanced years. And so, tall and spare, with his long flowing hair and in that attire, he looked like some patriarch and even more like the engraving of the poet Kukolnikov that was reproduced in the 1830 edition of his works. He resembled that engraving when he sat on a garden bench in the summer with a lilac bush behind him, leaning with both hands on his cane, an open book next to him, musing poetically over the setting sun.

Speaking of books, let me note here that toward the end he read less and less—but that was only toward the very end of his life. He always read the numerous newspapers and magazines to which Mrs. Stavrogin subscribed. He was also interested in the latest developments in Russian literature, although on that point he maintained a dignified reserve. At one time he embarked with great enthusiasm upon a study of our home and foreign policies, but soon gave it up with a shrug. He also sometimes went into the garden carrying Tocqueville in his hand, but with a sentimental Paul de Kock novel concealed in his pocket. But all that is unimportant.

Now let me say, parenthetically, a few words about Kukolnikov's portrait too. Varvara Stavrogin had come across it when she was a little girl in an exclusive Moscow boarding school. She immediately fell in love with it, girls in boarding schools having a propensity for falling in love with anyone and anything, including their teachers—particularly teachers of penmanship and drawing. However, what concerns us here is not what sort of little girl Mrs. Stavrogin was but the fact that even at the age of fifty she still preserved that picture among her other intimate treasures. This may explain why she made Mr. Verkhovensky dress the way she did. But that, of course, is also immaterial.

During the first years of his stay at Mrs. Stavrogin's, Mr. Verkhovensky still intended to write a book. In fact, he was about to start on it every day. But, in later years, he must have forgotten whatever it was he had had in mind. More and more frequently he said:

"I feel I'm ready to begin work. I have all the necessary materials at hand, yet—somehow I can't get started."

And he lowered his head in despair.

Of course, the pangs of scholarly creation he suffered added to his glamour in our eyes, although he himself thirsted for something different.

"They've forgotten about me! No one needs me any more!" he often exclaimed.

This despair became particularly intense toward the end of the eighteen fifties, and Mrs. Stavrogin finally realized that it was sincere. She couldn't bear the idea that her old friend was forgotten and useless. To distract him and refurbish his glory, she took him on a trip to Moscow, where she still had a few elegant literary and learned acquaintances. But the Moscow trip turned out to be rather unsatisfactory.

It was a strange time: something was in the air—something very different from the old, settled calm; something quite unfamiliar that could nevertheless be scented all over the place, even in Skvoreshniki. All kinds of rumors were reaching us. The facts were, by and large, well known, but there were all sorts of ideas surrounding those facts—indeed, an oversaturation of ideas. And that was what was bewildering: it was hard to accommodate oneself to those ideas or, indeed, grasp what they actually meant. Mrs. Stavrogin, being a woman, persisted in suspecting that there was something secret about them. She started to read foreign newspapers and magazines that she managed to obtain (although they were banned in Russia) as well as all sorts of clandestine pamphlets and proclamations. But she soon gave up, because they made her head spin. Then she started to write letters. But she received few replies, and even those she received were less and less intelligible as time went by.

So she solemnly asked Mr. Verkhovensky to explain "all those ideas" to her once and for all. When he was through, however, his explanations left her eminently dissatisfied. His views on the general commotion were exceedingly scornful. Everything, in his opinion, boiled down to the fact that they had forgotten him and that there was no room for him in the new movement.

In the end, however, they remembered him. First in émigré

publications abroad that recalled his exile and martyrdom, then in Petersburg, where he was described as a former star of a famous old constellation and compared—for some obscure reason—with Radishchev. Then someone reported his death and promised to send in an obituary. After that, Mr. Verkhovensky was immediately resurrected and reappeared filled with new importance. All his scorn for the politicians of the day vanished, and he became frantically anxious to go to Petersburg, join the new movement, and show his mettle.

Mrs. Stavrogin regained her old faith and got busy. They decided to leave for Petersburg without further delay, find out everything for themselves, and if possible, give themselves ungrudgingly and unstintingly to the new cause. She declared, by the way, that she was willing to publish a new magazine and devote the rest of her life to it. Seeing how important all this was to her, Mr. Verkhovensky became even more overbearing, and Mrs. Stavrogin soon detected a patronizing tone in his dealings with her, a fact of which she made immediate note.

It must be said, however, that she also pursued another objective in going to Petersburg—namely, the renewal of her old connections. She had to try her best to remind society of her existence.

But the ostensible reason for her trip was to see her only son, who was just then graduating from a Petersburg boarding school.

VI

So they went to Petersburg and stayed there for almost the entire winter season. By Lent, however, their hopes had burst like an iridescent soap bubble. Their dreams were shattered, and the foggy confusion, instead of clearing, became thicker and more sickening.

In the first place, Mrs. Stavrogin didn't succeed in reestablishing her connections, except perhaps on a ridiculously small scale—and that at the cost of the most humiliating efforts. Offended, she plunged wholeheartedly into the service of the "new ideas" and began organizing political evenings at home. She invited all sorts of literary figures, who were immediately shepherded into her drawing room in droves. After that they started coming without being invited—one would bring along another. She had never seen such men of letters before; they were incredibly but quite openly vain, as though in being so vain they were performing some sort of function. Some, though by no means all, arrived drunk and then behaved as if there were something beautiful in drunkenness that they had discovered only yesterday. Indeed, they all seemed proud of something. Their faces proclaimed that they had just this minute discovered some terribly important secret. They swore at one another and admired themselves for doing so. It was difficult to find out what they had actually written, but they described themselves as critics, novelists, satirists, playwrights, and debunkers.

Mr. Verkhovensky managed to penetrate to their top layer, their ruling clique. He climbed an incredible distance to reach those who were actually at the controls, but they received him warmly. Of course, none of them had ever heard of him— they only gathered that he was for The Idea. And he maneuvered them so adroitly that, despite their exalted positions, he managed to get them to attend Mrs. Stavrogin's receptions once or twice. These men were very serious, polite, and well behaved, and the others seemed afraid of them. But apparently they didn't have too much time to spare. Two or three former literary lions with whom Mrs. Stavrogin had managed to maintain graceful relations also turned up. But, to her amazement, these genuine celebrities behaved sheepishly before the new rabble and shamefully tried to curry favor with them.

At first Mr. Verkhovensky was lucky. They used him as a sort of exhibit at literary gatherings. When he appeared for the first time on the dais at a public reading, he received a five-minute ovation. Even nine years later, the tears still sprang to his eyes when he remembered it—although those tears were due to artistic temperament rather than gratitude.

"I'd swear," he told me, although he insisted on secrecy, "I'd bet anything that none of that audience knew even the first thing about me!"

It is a terribly significant remark. On the one hand, it showed that he was intelligent and understood his position clearly, despite the state of exaltation he was then in. On the other hand, the fact that even nine years later he still couldn't think of it without trembling with resentment indicates that his intellect was not really so keen.

They insisted he sign two or three petitions protesting against something—he couldn't make out what. He signed. They also asked Mrs. Stavrogin to sign a protest against some "scandalous practice," and she did so.

Although most of the "new people" came to her house, they somehow felt obliged to look upon Mrs. Stavrogin sneeringly and with undisguised contempt. In moments of bitterness, Mr. Verkhovensky hinted to me that her jealousy of him dated from that time. She no doubt realized that she shouldn't associate with those people; nevertheless she received them very eagerly, with an almost hysterical, very feminine impatience. She obviously expected something from them. At her receptions she didn't say much, although she could have if she had chosen to. She preferred to listen.

They spoke of: abolition of censorship; the reform of spelling; substitution of the Roman alphabet for the Cyrillic; the recent exile of such-and-such; some scandal in the fashionable shopping center; the advantages of breaking up the Russian Empire into autonomous ethnic units united by freely accepted federal ties; abolition of the army and navy; the restoration to Poland of land up to the Dnieper; agrarian reform; abolition of inheritance, family, parental rights, and priests; women's rights; the scandalously luxurious mansion belonging to a certain Mr. Krayevsky, for which they couldn't forgive him; and so on.

Among these newcomers there were obviously a number of crooks. However, most of the others were honest, even good, people, although sometimes of astounding shades of opinion. Of course, the honest ones were much harder to understand than the obviously dishonest and the cynically rude, but it was impossible to tell who was using whom for what purpose.

When Mrs. Stavrogin revealed her intention of publishing a magazine, a new flood of people rushed to her receptions. But immediately many of them openly accused her of being a capitalist and exploiting labor. The rudeness of these accusations was only equaled by their complete unexpectedness.

Once the elderly General Drozdov, a friend and colleague of the late General Stavrogin's and a pleasant man in his way—we all knew him here—although very stubborn and irritable, a big eater, and an inveterate foe of atheism—once, at one of those receptions, he got into a heated argument with some famous youth.

"If you talk like that, you must be a general," the young man told him to clinch an argument, implying that he couldn't think of any more derogatory word than "general."

General Drozdov flew into a terrible rage.

"Yes sir, I am a general—a lieutenant general, to be precise, and I have served my tsar loyally, whereas you're nothing but a milksop and an atheist!"

An intolerable commotion followed, and the following day the incident was reported in the press. A petition was circulated protesting "the disgraceful attitude of Mrs. Stavrogin" in refusing to have the general thrown out there and then. There was also a cartoon in an illustrated magazine. It represented Mrs. Stavrogin, General Drozdov, and Mr. Verkhovensky beneath the caption: "Three Reactionary Bedfellows"; and under the cartoon there was a satirical verse written especially for the occasion by "a poet of the people."

I must note here that many generals do have a strange way of expressing themselves. For instance, they say things like "I've served *my* tsar . . ." as if they had a tsar of their own and not the same tsar as the rest of us, their common compatriots.

Remaining in Petersburg any longer was, of course, unthinkable. Besides, Mr. Verkhovensky finally proved a complete failure. He couldn't restrain himself and started defending the rights of Art. They laughed at him louder than ever. At the final gathering, he decided to touch them with his revolutionary eloquence, hoping to reach their hearts, figuring to gain their sympathy by mentioning his years "in exile." He accepted unquestioningly the uselessness, the ridiculous connotation of the notion "mother country"; he endorsed the theory that religion was harmful; but he declared loudly and proudly that he placed Pushkin's poems above shoes—very much so. They booed him so mercilessly that he dissolved into tears right there on the stage. Mrs. Stavrogin took him home more dead than alive.

"They treated me like an old nightcap," he kept moaning.

She sat with him the whole night, made him take sedative drops, and until daybreak kept whispering in his ear:

"You're still useful . . . you'll prove yourself yet . . . they'll still appreciate you . . . in some other place."

The next day, Mrs. Stavrogin received a visit from five men of letters, three of whom she'd never seen or heard of before. With very stern expressions on their faces, they informed her that they had studied the matter of her publication and had reached a decision. Mrs. Stavrogin had never asked anyone to study or decide anything about her projected publication. Their decision was that once she had founded the magazine, she should hand it over to them, together with the funds for running it, on a free, cooperative basis, and immediately retire to Skvoreshniki, taking with her Stepan Verkhovensky, who had become "definitely behind the times." Out of special consideration for her, they were willing to recognize her rights of ownership and send her one-sixth of the annual net profits—if there were any. And the most touching part of it all was that four of these five people were pursuing absolutely no gainful end in this transaction, but were acting only in the interest of the Cause.

"We left Petersburg in a complete daze," Mr. Verkhovensky told me. "I didn't understand any of it and kept muttering some nonsense to the rumble of the train:

> Bang, bing, kick 'em out,
> Kick 'em out, bang, bing . . .

"And on and on, all the way to Moscow. I only recovered when we reached Moscow—as if I expected to find things different in that city."

"Ah, my dear friends!" he sometimes exclaimed to us, inspired, "you have no idea how sad, how bitter one feels when a great idea to which you have devoted your life is taken over by inexperienced, clumsy hands that drag it out into the street and share it with other fools as stupid as themselves. Then you suddenly come across it in the flea market, unrecognizable, grimy, presented from a ridiculous angle, without sense of proportion, without harmony, used as a toy by stupid brats. Oh no, it was different in our time! That's not what we were trying to achieve. No, no, that's not at all what we were after! I don't recognize anything today. . . . But our time will come again and set a firm course and put an end to today's swerving. It must. Otherwise where will we wind up?"

VII

Immediately upon their return from Petersburg, Mrs. Stavrogin packed her friend off abroad "to recuperate a bit." Besides, she felt they had to have a little rest from each other. Mr. Verkhovensky left enthusiastically.

"I'll come back to life there," he declared. "I'll return to my studies there!"

But his very first letters from Berlin were of the usual tenor. "My heart is shattered," he wrote Mrs. Stavrogin. "I cannot forget! Here in Berlin, everything reminds me of the old days, the first joys and sufferings. Where is she? Where are they both today? Where are those two angelic women of whom I was never worthy? Where is my son, my dearly beloved son? And where am I, my former self, made of steel and unshakable as a rock? How is it that, today, someone called Andreyev, a bearded Russian-Orthodox fool, can break my whole life in two?" . . .

Now Mr. Verkhovensky had seen his son only twice in his life—when he was born, and recently in Petersburg, where the young man had just entered the university. Until then, as we mentioned, the boy had been brought up by some aunts (Mrs. Stavrogin provided for his upkeep) in a remote province far from Skvoreshniki. As to Andreyev, he was just an eccentric local shopkeeper who had taught himself archaeology and become a great collector of Russian antiques. He sometimes liked to challenge Mr. Verkhovensky's erudite statements and, even more so, his political beliefs. The shopkeeper, who looked very venerable with his white beard and silver-rimmed glasses, still owed Mr. Verkhovensky four hundred rubles for a few acres of timber he had bought from Mr. Verkhovensky's small estate near Skvoreshniki. Although Mrs. Stavrogin had supplied him with lavish funds for his trip, Mr. Verkhovensky had reckoned on those four hundred rubles to pay for some things he felt (probably secretly) he needed and he almost burst into tears when Andreyev asked him to wait another month. Actually, Andreyev was perfectly entitled to do this, since he had made the first payments almost six months in advance because Mr. Verkhovensky apparently had been in urgent need of money at that time too.

Mrs. Stavrogin eagerly read that first letter and underlined in pencil the words, "where are they both today?" Then she folded it, dated it, and locked it in her metal box. He was, of course, referring to his late wives.

The second letter from Berlin was a variation on the same theme.

"I am working twelve hours a day"—"I'd have settled for eleven," Mrs. Stavrogin muttered—"I am digging up material in the libraries, checking, comparing, copying passages, rushing around, seeing various professors. I have renewed my acquaintance with the Dundasov family. Such nice people. Mrs. Dundasov is still as lovely as ever. She sends you her regards. Her young husband and three nephews are all here in Berlin. I talk to the young people until dawn. We have parties here that might be described as Athenian, but only, of course, in the sense of being refined and intellectual and of high aesthetic quality. Everything is so beautiful: there is a lot of music, principally Spanish, and a great longing for the general regeneration of mankind. And there is the concept of eternal beauty, the Sistine Madonna, the alternation of light and shadow, with dark spots even on the sun! Ah, my dear, loyal, noble friend! My heart is with you, and I am always yours and with you alone *en tout pays* and even *dans le pays de Makar et ses veaux* of which, you may remember, we so often spoke, shudderingly, before we left Petersburg. The thought of it makes me smile now. Once across the border I felt safe at last—a strange, new sensation experienced for the first time in so many years . . ." etc.

"What nonsense!" was Mrs. Stavrogin's verdict as she folded this letter too. "If those Athenian evenings last until dawn, how can he possibly spend twelve hours a day over his books? Was he by any chance drunk when he wrote that? And how does that Dundasov woman dare send me her regards? But, after all, let him have his fling. . . ."

The sentence *dans le pays de Makar et ses veaux* stood for the Russian saying "Where Makar never drove his sheep"—i.e., Siberia. Mr. Verkhovensky was fond of translating all sorts of Russian sayings into French in the most idiotic way. Without doubt he could have translated them much better if he'd wanted to, but he thought it witty to distort them like that.

However, his fling didn't last very long. He could not take it for four full months and hurried back to Skvoreshniki. His later letters were composed of tender outpourings to his much-missed dearest friend; they were literally dampened with tears of separation. Some people become attached to their homes the way lap dogs do.

Their meeting was rapturous. But two days later, everything was just as before—in fact, even duller than before.

"My dear man," Mr. Verkhovensky said to me a couple of weeks later under a solemn oath of secrecy, "I must tell you, I've discovered a terrible thing—terrible for me, that is. . . .

Je suis un . . . nothing but a common hanger-on, *et rien de plus! Mais r-r-rien de plus!"*

VIII

Then things quieted down and remained quiet for almost nine years. The hysterical outbursts and sobbing on my shoulder that recurred at regular intervals didn't really disturb the calm atmosphere. I'm rather surprised that Mr. Verkhovensky didn't grow fat during that time. His nose turned a bit crimson and he himself grew even milder, but that was all. Gradually, he gathered a circle of friends around him, but—it must be said—it was always quite small. And although Mrs. Stavrogin had little to do with that circle, we all considered ourselves her protégés.

She had learned her lesson during her last stay in Petersburg and now definitely installed herself in our town. That is, she lived there in the winter and in the summer stayed on her nearby estate, Skvoreshniki. She never had so much weight and influence in our provincial society as during the last seven of those years—in fact, until our present governor was appointed. The former governor, our kindly, unforgettable Ivan Osipovich, was closely related to her, and once upon a time she had rendered him some important service. His wife trembled at the mere thought of displeasing Mrs. Stavrogin. So the adulation of our provincial society bordered at times on plain idolatry. Some of this glamour was, of course, reflected onto Stepan Verkhovensky. He was a member of the club and a stylish loser at cards, and was treated with general respect, although many thought him nothing but a "learned man."

Later, when Mrs. Stavrogin allowed him to live in a separate house, we felt freer. We gathered at his place twice a week and we enjoyed ourselves, especially when he was generous with the champagne. It came, by the way, from the shop of that fellow Andreyev whom we have already mentioned. Mrs. Stavrogin paid the bills every six months, and on those days Mr. Verkhovensky always had an upset stomach.

One of the earliest members of the circle was Liputin, a middle-aged official in the provincial administration, a great liberal with a reputation as an atheist in the town. He lived with his good-looking wife, who had brought him a handsome

dowry and had three grown-up daughters. He kept his family
terrorized and shut up at home; he was incredibly stingy and
had managed to amass enough money to acquire a house and
a bit of capital during his career as a public servant. He was
a cantankerous character, and since he was also of modest
station in life, he was little respected in the town and not
even received in top society. He was, moreover, a notoriously
malicious gossip, and at least twice had been chastised for
his slanders—once by an officer and once by a landowner, the
respected father of a family. But we liked his keen wit, his
inquiring mind, and his talent for vicious jibes. Mrs. Stavrogin
didn't like him, but he always managed to get around her.

Nor did she have much love for Shatov, who had joined
our group only a year or so before. Shatov was a former university student who had been expelled from the university
after some scandal. As a boy, he had been one of Mr. Verkhovensky's pupils. He was a serf by birth, the son of Mrs.
Stavrogin's late valet, Pavel. She had done a lot for him, but
now she disliked him because she considered him ungrateful
and she couldn't forgive him for not coming straight to her
when he was expelled from the university. As a matter of
fact, he didn't even answer the letter she wrote him at the
time; instead he sold himself to some enlightened merchant
as tutor to his children. He accompanied the merchant's family
abroad, performing the functions of a nurse rather than a
tutor—but then, he was anxious to go abroad at the time. Just
before they left on the trip, the merchant took on a governess
for the children, an energetic Russian girl hired mostly because
she was willing to accept such a modest salary. Within a
couple of months, she was fired by the merchant for "free
thinking." Shatov left and followed her to Geneva, where
they were married. They lived together for about three weeks,
then parted like free people, without obligations toward each
other—although poverty was also a factor in their separation.
After that, Shatov wandered about Europe by himself for a
long time, living God knows how, polishing shoes in the street,
working as a stevedore in seaports. Finally, about a year before,
he had returned to his home town and gone to live with an
old aunt, whom he buried a month later. Shatov had a sister
called Dasha who had been brought up by Mrs. Stavrogin and
whom that lady now liked very much and treated as an equal.
But he had very little contact with her. Among us he was
rather gloomy and taciturn, and when someone attacked his

convictions he became morbidly irritated and unrestrained in his language.

"Tie Shatov up first, and then argue," Mr. Verkhovensky used to quip. But he was rather fond of him.

When abroad, Shatov radically altered his former socialist convictions and jumped to the other extreme. He was one of those Russian idealists who, once struck by some overwhelming idea, becomes obsessed by it, sometimes for the rest of his life. He cannot ever really grasp it, but he believes in it passionately, and his life becomes an uninterrupted series of agonizing pangs, as if he were half crushed by a heavy stone.

Physically, Shatov fitted his convictions very well: he was clumsy, towheaded, unkempt, short, big-shouldered, with blond, almost white, bushy eyebrows. His permanent frown and obstinately lowered eyes made him always look embarrassed about something. On his head one particular tuft of hair never flattened down but always stuck up like some plant. He was twenty-seven or twenty-eight.

"No wonder his wife deserted him," Mrs. Stavrogin said once, giving him a thorough looking over.

Shatov always tried to dress neatly despite his extreme poverty. He never asked Mrs. Stavrogin for help, managing as well as he could by doing odd jobs for the local merchants. At one point, he actually clerked in a grocery; at another, he was supposed to sail off on a river boat with a load of merchandise, but fell ill just before leaving. It is hard to imagine the poverty he could stand without even giving it a thought. After his sickness, Mrs. Stavrogin sent him a hundred rubles anonymously. He found out, however, who had sent the money, mulled over what he should do, decided to accept it, and went over to thank her. She received him with overwhelming warmth, but even on this occasion Shatov managed to disappoint her and disgrace himself: he stayed only five minutes and didn't say a word. He kept staring at the floor with a stupid, frozen smile; then, at the most interesting point in her speech, he suddenly rose without waiting for her to finish her sentence, nodded awkwardly without looking at her, and totally confused, stumbled against her expensive inlaid sewing table, which tipped over, fell, and broke. Finally, dead with shame, he rushed out.

Liputin often reproached him after that for having accepted the hundred rubles from that despotic woman, a former serf owner, and for not only accepting them but even trotting over there to thank her.

Shatov lived at the edge of town and kept very much to himself; he didn't like any of us to come and see him. But he came regularly to Mr. Verkhovensky's gatherings and borrowed books and newspapers from him.

There was another young man who came to our gatherings. He was a young local official called Virginsky. In some ways he was a bit like Shatov, although in others he seemed as different from him as it was possible to be. He was what is known as "a family man." He was a very sad young man (actually he was already past thirty) and well educated, although mostly self-taught. He was poor, married, and worked in a department of the local administration; he also supported his wife's aunt and sister. His wife and the other two ladies held the most progressive political views, which, however, they formulated rather crudely—an illustration of what Mr. Verkhovensky meant when he spoke on some occasions of "ideas that get caught up in the street." They took everything they read literally, and at a hint from progressive circles in the capital, they'd have tossed out of their windows everything they were advised to toss out. In our town, Mrs. Virginsky practiced as a midwife. Before her marriage, she had lived for a long time in Petersburg.

Virginsky himself was a man of exceptional purity of heart, and I have never come across a set of more passionately held convictions.

"Never, never will I give up these bright hopes!" he told me with shining eyes.

He always spoke of these "bright hopes" quietly, almost in a whisper, as if he were mentioning something secret.

He was quite tall, but very thin, and his shoulders were strikingly narrow. His hair had a reddish tinge and was growing thin. He took Mr. Verkhovensky's jibes at some of his opinions meekly, but when he answered him, he spoke very seriously, often leaving Mr. Verkhovensky speechless. Mr. Verkhovensky treated him kindly and paternally—as, for that matter, he treated us all.

"You're just a half-baked thinker," he teased Virginsky. "You're all the same! And, although I haven't noticed the same narrowness of outlook in you that I found *chez ces séminaristes* of Petersburg, I still maintain you're half-baked.

And Shatov is half-baked too, however well done he may imagine he is."

"And what about me?" Liputin asked him once.

"You're just a middle-of-the-roader; you'll always adapt yourself somehow to whatever may come."

Liputin resented this.

It was rumored and, alas, turned out to be true that, after less than a year of lawful wedlock, Mrs. Virginsky dismissed her husband, announcing that she preferred a certain Lebyatkin. The person in question later turned out to be a rather suspicious character and not the retired army captain he had posed as. He was only good at twirling his mustache, drinking, and talking the most cockeyed nonsense imaginable. He rather tactlessly moved right into the Virginsky household, welcoming the opportunity for free board. He slept there, ate there, and in the end, started treating the master of the house quite patronizingly. When told about his dismissal by his wife, Virginsky is supposed to have said:

"My dear, thus far I have only loved you; now I respect you."

But it is highly unlikely he ever made this statement so much in the style of ancient Rome. I've heard from other sources that he burst into tears.

Once, a couple of weeks after the dismissal, the whole "family" went to have tea with some friends outside town. Virginsky was rather exuberant and gay and took part in the dancing. Then, suddenly, without any provocation, he grabbed the gigantic Lebyatkin, who was dancing a solo, by his hair, bent him forward, and screaming and shouting, with the tears pouring down his cheeks, started pulling him around. The giant was so scared that he did nothing to defend himself and didn't even utter a sound while he was being dragged around. Later, however, he ardently resented the offense, as any honorable man would.

Virginsky spent the following night on his knees, begging his wife to forgive him. But she didn't, for he still refused to apologize to Lebyatkin. And on top of that, she accused him of shallowness of conviction and stupidity for kneeling while talking to a woman.

The retired captain vanished from our town soon afterward to reappear only very recently with his sister and a new set of objectives to which we'll come in time.

So it was no wonder that the wretched "family man" sought

refuge among us and needed our companionship. However, he never mentioned his family affairs in public. Only once, when the two of us were going home from Mr. Verkhovensky's place, did he say something vague about his unhappiness, but then he immediately seized my arm and said heatedly:

"Ah, it's nothing but a private matter that can in no way interfere with the common cause!"

Other people occasionally came to our meetings. There was a Jew named Lyamshin and a Captain Kartuzov. There was an open-minded old man, but he soon died. Once Liputin brought in an exiled Polish priest called Sloczewski, who was received as a matter of principle at first, but later on was no longer welcome.

IX

There was a time when it was said that our circle was a hotbed of freethinking, vice, and atheism, and this notion always lingered about us. But in actual fact we were just enjoying a pleasant, innocent Russian pastime—liberal blather. Liberal idealism and liberal idealists are possible only in Russia. Mr. Verkhovensky, like every witty man, needed an audience, and he also had to feel that he fulfilled a supreme duty by spreading ideas through words. Finally, he obviously needed someone to sip champagne with while exchanging a certain brand of pleasant Russian ideas about Russia, God in general, and the "Russian God" in particular, repeating for the hundredth time scandalous little jibes against the Russian authorities that everyone knew by heart. We didn't turn our noses up at local gossip, either, and often drew the most highly moral conclusions from it. We also frequently drifted into matters concerning mankind as a whole, discussing the future of Europe and the fate of man, forecasting dogmatically that Caesarism would reduce France to a second-rate power, a thing we were certain was imminent. The pope, we felt sure, would become just another cardinal in a unified Italy, and there wasn't the slightest doubt in our minds that this thousand-year-old matter would be settled with a snap of the fingers in our age of humanitarianism, industry, and railroads.

But then, idealistic Russian liberals had the same easy approach to everything.

Sometimes Mr. Verkhovensky spoke of art, and he spoke very well on the subject, although somewhat abstractly. At times he remembered the companions of his young days—all of them famous in the history of our movement—and he remembered them warmly and admiringly, but perhaps with a suggestion of envy. And if things became really unbearably boring, Lyamshin, the little Jewish post-office clerk, sat down at the piano and played, or gave imitations of a pig, a storm, a childbirth (including the infant's first cry), etc.—which was mostly why he was invited. And when we had had a lot to drink—which didn't happen very often—we were sufficiently moved to sing the *Marseillaise* together, with Lyamshin accompanying us on the piano. I can't guarantee that the result was very successful.

We enthusiastically celebrated February 18th, the day of the emancipation of the serfs, preparing for it long in advance by drinking innumerable toasts.

Long before Shatov and Virginsky joined us, when Mr. Verkhovensky was still living in Mrs. Stavrogin's house (it was some time before Emancipation), Mr. Verkhovensky had acquired the bad habit of muttering under his breath a well-known, although somewhat unconvincing, verse by some liberal ex-landowner:

> With their axes the peasants come walking,
> A terrible doom the land is stalking.

It went something like that, although I can't vouch for my accuracy.

Mrs. Stavrogin overheard him once, and shouting, "What stupid nonsense!" left the room in anger. Liputin, who happened to be present, remarked bitingly:

"Well, it would really be a shame if, in their joy, the peasants caused some unpleasantness to their former owners."

And he meaningfully drew his finger across his throat.

"Cher ami," Mr. Verkhovensky said good-humoredly, "take my word for it that this"—he imitated the gesture across the throat—"is no way to reform the landowners or help anyone else. We'll never manage to get things going if we lose our heads, although at times our heads do seem to be a positive hindrance."

I must say that many in our town expected something extraordinary to happen the day serfdom was abolished. Liputin and the so-called experts on people and the running of a state predicted it. Mr. Verkhovensky also seemed to share their opinion, and as the day approached, he begged Mrs. Stavrogin to send him abroad. In fact, he got cold feet. But the great day came and went and a few more days besides, and the haughty smile reappeared on Mr. Verkhovensky's lips. He formulated a few remarkable thoughts on the character of the Russian in general and the Russian peasant in particular.

"Being in a hurry as usual, we have been overanxious about our peasants. We have made them fashionable. A whole section of our literature has fussed about them as if they were some newly discovered precious stones. We've crowned their lice-infested heads with laurels, while in reality, in the past thousand years all we've got out of the Russian village is the Komarinsky Dance. Once a great Russian poet, who at the same time had some sense of humor, exclaimed, on seeing the great Rachel on the stage for the first time: 'I wouldn't exchange Rachel for a Russian peasant!' I'm prepared to go even further than that: I would give all the peasants in Russia for one Rachel. Let's face things soberly and stop mistaking our homemade grease for cleaning boots with *Le Bouquet de L'Impératrice* perfume."

Liputin readily agreed, but remarked that it was nevertheless necessary to pretend for the time being and praise the peasants in the interests of the Cause. He pointed out that even ladies of the highest society had shed hot tears over Grigorovich's story, "Anton the Sufferer," and some of them had even written from Paris to their estate managers back home, telling them that henceforth they were to treat the serfs as humanely as possible.

It was a rather unfortunate coincidence that, just after all those rumors started circulating about Anton Petrov, there was a certain misunderstanding in our province about ten miles from Skvoreshniki, and in the excitement they sent a detachment of soldiers this way. At that time Mr. Verkhovensky became so agitated that he gave us all a good scare. He ranted and raved at the club, saying that they hadn't sent enough soldiers and that we should wire for reinforcements; he rushed to the governor to assure him he had nothing to do with the whole business, insisting that they shouldn't try to accuse him of anything because of his old record and suggesting that the governor write immediately to whomever it might concern in the capital. Luckily, the whole incident soon blew over. Still, Mr. Verkhovensky's behavior struck me as very strange.

Three years later people started to discuss nationalism, and something called "public opinion" came into existence. That made Stepan Verkhovensky laugh.

"My friends," he lectured us, "if national consciousness has really come into existence among us, as we're told by the press, it is still attending some German elementary school and learning from a German textbook—learning by heart its eternal German lesson, and the German teacher can make it go down on its knees whenever he thinks fit. I have nothing against the German teacher. But I'm not so sure that this national feeling does exist today. I don't believe anything has come into existence; I think everything just goes on according to God's will—which should be good enough *pour notre Sainte Russie*. All these Pan-Slav and nationalist movements are really too old to be new. As a matter of fact, nationalism in this country has never been anything but a game for some gentlemen's club— and a Moscow club at that. Of course, I'm not talking of the times of Prince Igor. But finally, I say that its true origin is idleness. In our country everything comes from idleness, the good things as well. Everything comes from the cultured, refined idleness of our upper classes. I've been repeating this for thirty thousand years.

"Besides, we don't know how to live by our own labor. So why are they making all this fuss about some nascent 'public opinion'? What has happened? Did it fall suddenly from the sky? Can't they see that to have an opinion, people have to work themselves, have their own initiative, and have personal experience? No one gets anything for nothing. When we all work, we shall have our own opinions. And since we'll never go to work, those who work in our stead will make up our minds for us—the same old Europe, the same Germans, our teachers for two hundred years. Moreover, Russia is in too great a mess for us to disentangle it without the Germans and without going to work. For instance, I sounded the alarm and appealed to people to go to work. I devoted my life to that appeal and I believed in it, fool that I was! Now I don't believe any longer, but I keep pulling the rope of the alarm bell, and I'll go on ringing until the bell tolls my own requiem."

Alas, we went along with him. We applauded our teacher— and with what enthusiasm! But then, don't we still hear all around us the same "nice," "clever," old Russian nonsense?

Our teacher did believe in God.

"I don't know why everyone around here insists I'm an atheist," he said. "I believe in God—but let's make a distinction: I believe in God as a being that is conscious of Himself only through me. Of course, I cannot believe like my old maid, or like some gentleman who believes just in case, or like our dear Shatov . . . but no—Shatov doesn't really count. Shatov *forces* himself to believe, like a Moscow Slavophile. As to Christianity, well, despite all my respect for it, I'm not a Christian. I'm rather a pagan like the great Goethe or the ancient Greeks, if only because Christianity doesn't understand woman, a point that was so brilliantly developed by George Sand in one of her great novels. As for genuflections, fasts, and that sort of thing, I fail to understand what difference it can make to anyone whether or not I observe them. I can imagine how busy our local informers are, but I refuse to be a hypocrite. In 1847 Belinsky sent his well-publicized letter to Gogol from abroad, strongly reproaching him for believing in 'some sort of God.' *Entre nous soit dit,* I can imagine nothing funnier than Gogol—the Gogol of *that* time especially—reading that particular phrase and the letter in general! But disregarding the funny side of it, and since, after all, I agree in principle with that reproach, I'll simply say: there were real men at that time! Yes, they knew how to love their people, how to suffer for them. They were willing to sacrifice everything for the masses and at the same time managed to remain distinct from them, not trying to please them in everything. But you don't really expect Belinsky to try to find salvation in lean diets of vegetable oil, radishes, and peas during Lent!"

At this point Shatov intervened.

"Those fellows you mentioned never really loved the people; they never suffered for them or sacrificed anything for them, although to make themselves feel more noble they liked to think they did," he muttered gloomily, lowering his eyes and twisting impatiently in his chair.

"What? You say they didn't love the people?" Mr. Verkhovensky shouted in outraged tones. "You don't know what you're talking about! They loved the people! Most certainly!"

"They loved neither the people nor Russia!" Shatov yelled back, his eyes flashing. "It's impossible to love something you know nothing about, and they didn't know a damn thing about the Russian people! All of you, including yourself, and especially Belinsky, had just the most cursory glimpse of the Rus-

sian people. You can see that from his letter to Gogol alone.
Belinsky is just like the fellow in Krylov's fable who, when he
visited a menagerie, spent his time marveling at some French
social insects and so managed to overlook the elephants. He
began and ended with those bugs! Even so, I'd say Belinsky
was cleverer than the lot of you. As to the rest of you, you've
not only failed to look at the Russian masses, but treated them
with scornful distaste, judging by the fact that by 'people'
you've always understood the French people, and at that, only
the people of Paris, and you're ashamed that the Russian people aren't like them. That's the truth! And a man who has no
country has no God either. Rest assured that those who cease
to understand the people of their own country and lose contact with them also lose the faith of their forefathers and become godless or indifferent. Yes, yes, it always proves true;
that's why you and the lot of us today are either despicable
atheists or indifferent, vicious human muck. Yes, Mr. Verkhovensky, you too. I make no exception of you! As a matter
of fact, I was thinking of you when I said all that."

Having delivered his speech (a thing he did from time to
time), Shatov as usual grabbed his cap and rushed to the door,
convinced that now his friendship with Mr. Verkhovensky
was finally ended.

But Mr. Verkhovensky always managed to stop him in time.

"All right, Shatov," he said good-humoredly, offering him
his hand without rising from his armchair, "now, how about
making up after that exchange of niceties?"

Awkward and self-conscious, Shatov hated sentimental
effusions. Outwardly abrupt and uncouth, he was, I believe,
secretly an extremely sensitive man, and although he often lost
all sense of proportion, he himself was the first to suffer from
it. So, after making some grunting noises over Mr. Verkhovensky's suggestion and shuffling his feet like a bear for a
while, he suddenly grinned, put down his cap, and sat down—
all without once raising his eyes from the floor. Of course, on
these occasions, wine was brought in, and Mr. Verkhovensky
proposed some appropriate toast, usually to one of the great
social fighters of the past.

chapter 2

PRINCE HAL—MATCHMAKING

I

The other person in the world to whom Varvara Petrovna Stavrogin was as attached as to Mr. Verkhovensky was her only son, Nikolai Vsevolodovich Stavrogin. It was for him that Mr. Verkhovensky had been invited to come as tutor. Nikolai was eight at the time. His irresponsible father was already living apart from them, and the boy was entirely in his mother's care.

In fairness to Mr. Verkhovensky, it must be said that he knew how to gain the affection of his pupil. His secret was quite simple: he was a child himself. I wasn't around then, and since he always needed a confidant, he didn't hesitate to make a friend out of even such a small child, and as the boy grew, any gap that may have existed between them seemed to disappear. He repeatedly woke his ten- or eleven-year-old friend in the middle of the night and tearfully poured out his wounded sensibilities or even shared some family secret with him, which, of course, was quite unforgivable. Then they would sob in each other's arms.

The boy knew his mother loved him, but he didn't seem to feel very much for her. She didn't talk to him much and hardly ever prevented him from doing what he wanted, but somehow he felt the intensity with which she watched him, and that made him painfully ill at ease. In any case, Mrs. Stavrogin fully entrusted Mr. Verkhovensky with her son's education, as well as the building of his character.

We may assume that the tutor was to some extent responsible for upsetting his pupil's nerves, for when the boy was sent to boarding school at the age of fifteen, he was puny, pale, and strangely withdrawn. (Later, however, he was noted for his remarkably powerful physique. We may assume that the two friends' tears, when they sobbed in each other's arms at night, were not always caused by domestic intrigues. Mr. Verkhovensky had managed to touch the deepest-seated chords in the boy's heart, causing the first, still undefined, sensation of the undying, sacred longing that a superior soul, having once tasted, will never exchange for vulgar satisfaction. (There are even people who value that longing more than the most radical fulfillment, even when it is possible.)

Anyway, it seemed a good idea finally to separate the teacher and his pupil, even though it was rather late.

During his first two years at boarding school, young Stavrogin came home for the summer holidays. Then, when his mother and Mr. Verkhovensky went to stay in Petersburg, he sometimes attended their literary parties, looking and listening. He didn't talk much and was shy and quiet, as he had been before. He still treated Mr. Verkhovensky with tender affection, but was more reserved and obviously reluctant to discuss with him lofty matters or, for that matter, the past.

In compliance with his mother's wishes, after graduating from school he joined one of the most elegant Horse Guards regiments. However, he didn't go home to let his mother admire him in uniform as she suggested and wrote only seldom after that.

Mrs. Stavrogin sent her son all the money he wanted, despite the fact that, immediately after the emancipation of the serfs, her income was cut by about half. But then, it must be said, she had managed to accumulate a bit of capital and could probably afford it. She was very eager for her son to be a social success, and she was not disappointed. Where she had failed in renewing her connections, the rich young Guards officer succeeded easily. In fact, he established connections that she wouldn't have dared dream of. Everyone was delighted to receive him.

But strange rumors soon began to reach Mrs. Stavrogin. Her son apparently had suddenly plunged into the wildest dissipation. It was nothing like the usual drinking and gambling. The reports cited savage recklessness, people run down by his horses, and his unspeakably brutal behavior toward a lady of the highest society with whom he had an affair and whom he then insulted publicly. There was something obviously unnatural about it all. Apparently he had become a terrible bully and went around insulting people for the sheer joy of it. Mrs. Stavrogin was worried and depressed. Mr. Verkhovensky tried to assure her that it was just the growing pangs of a richly endowed and highly complex nature, that the stormy seas would calm down, and that her son's youth resembled Prince

Hal's, whose mad revels with Falstaff, Poins, and Mistress Quickly Shakespeare describes in *Henry IV, Part 1*.

Mrs. Stavrogin didn't just brush him aside with a "Rubbish, rubbish!" as she had tended to recently. On the contrary, she listened to him intently and asked him to tell her more about Shakespeare. Then she read the play herself. But Shakespeare's drama didn't reassure her—she couldn't find the least similarity between the two cases. Meanwhile, she eagerly awaited her son's reply to several letters of hers.

However, her questions were soon answered. She received the sinister news that her Prince Hal had been involved in two duels, one right after the other, in both of which he had been in the wrong. He had killed one of his opponents and maimed the other. He was court-martialed, reduced to the ranks, and transferred to an infantry regiment. Indeed, only special intercession from above saved him from a sterner sentence.

In 1863 he somehow managed to distinguish himself. They gave him a medal and promoted him to corporal. Then, in a surprisingly short time, they gave him back his commission.

During that whole period, Mrs. Stavrogin must have sent a hundred letters to the capital with pleas for special consideration. In this special instance she was willing to humble herself.

But, soon after he regained his commission, the young man suddenly resigned it and left the army. However, he did not return to Skvoreshniki; indeed, he ceased to write to his mother altogether. Later she found out circumspectly that he was back in Petersburg but he was never seen with his former acquaintances any more. He apparently was avoiding them. Finally, she discovered that he kept strange company, associating with the dregs of Petersburg; that he went around with penniless petty employees, drunks, and retired army officers who stooped to "dignified" begging in the street. It was said that he visited their filthy homes, spent days and nights in slums and God knows what grimy alleys; that he had let himself go, looked like a tramp, and apparently liked it that way.

He never asked his mother for money. He had inherited a small estate from his father that yielded a little income, for he had rented it to some German from Saxony. His mother at last succeeded in persuading him to come to see her, and Prince Hal appeared in our town. That was the first time I ever saw him.

He was a strikingly handsome man of about twenty-five, and

I must confess, he greatly impressed me. I expected to find a shabby tramp, debilitated by debauchery and reeking of vodka. But what I saw was the most elegant gentleman I'd ever met: he was dressed in the best of taste and behaved as only those accustomed to the most refined surroundings behave. And I was not the only one to be surprised—the whole town was, for everyone knew young Stavrogin's story, including details the knowledge of which was surprising. (And, even more surprising, a good half of these turned out to be correct.)

The new arrival immediately captured the attention of our local ladies. They split into two opposing groups: one adoring, the other crying for his blood. But all of them were fascinated by him. Some were attracted because they felt there was some mystery about him; others were positively thrilled by the thought that he was a killer. He also turned out to be rather well educated, even well informed. Of course, it didn't take much information to impress us, but he had enough to speak with competence on the great topics of the day, and what's more, he did so calmly, trying to make good sense. Curiously enough, from the first day of his arrival, we found him an extremely reasonable man.

He was elegant without affectation, not too talkative, very modest, and at the same time bold and self-reliant. There was no one like him around. Our local lions, full of envy, were pushed into the background.

I was also struck by his looks. His handsome head of black hair was somehow a bit too black, his light eyes were perhaps too steady, his complexion too smooth and delicate, and his cheeks too rosy and healthy; his teeth were like pearls and his lips like coral. This sounds like a strikingly beautiful face, but in reality it was repulsive rather than beautiful. His face reminded some people of a mask. There was also much talk about his great physical strength. He was of above-average height. His mother regarded him with pride, but also with constant worry. He spent six months with us. At first he was quiet, distant, and reserved. He attended social functions and rigidly adhered to etiquette. He was related to the governor through his father, and was received in the governor's mansion like one of the family.

Then the beast suddenly unsheathed his claws.

I must remark here that our former governor, dear old Ivan Osipovich, rather resembled an old woman—but a well-born old woman with good connections, which accounts for his remaining so long in office while always managing to dodge work and responsibility. His hospitality and amiability might have qualified him to be chairman of the local gentry association in the peaceful old days, but certainly not to be governor in our troubled times. People often said that it was Mrs. Stavrogin, not the governor, who ran our province. This, however, was nothing but a catty and absolutely unfounded remark. And indeed, too many people have exercised their wit on that subject. Actually, in recent years, Mrs. Stavrogin had deliberately withdrawn from among those in control and, despite her tremendous prestige in high society, she voluntarily remained within the strict limits she had set for herself. Instead of high politics, she had concentrated on running her estates and, within two or three years, had succeeded in raising her income almost to what it had been before Emancipation. Instead of making the romantic gestures of the past—such as the trip to Petersburg and the idea of founding a liberal magazine —she cut her expenses and started saving. She even decided to separate from Mr. Verkhovensky, allowing him to rent an apartment in another house, something that, under various pretexts, he had been asking her to let him do for a long time. Little by little, Mr. Verkhovensky started describing her as down-to-earth, referring to her facetiously as "my down-to-earth friend." Of course, he only indulged in jokes of this sort with great discretion and under suitable circumstances.

All of us who knew her well—and Mr. Verkhovensky better than any of us—understood that her son now represented her new hopes and even a new daydream of hers. Her great love for her son dated from the time of his success in Petersburg society and grew immensely when he was stripped of his commission and reduced to the ranks. But at the same time she seemed to be afraid of him and behaved rather slavishly toward him. She obviously feared something ill defined and mysterious, something she herself couldn't pinpoint. She often watched him discreetly and intently, trying to decipher and understand something. . . .

Then the beast unsheathed his claws.

II

Suddenly, without any provocation, our prince committed several unprecedented outrages, different from anything one would have imagined, not at all the usual run-of-the-mill things. These were completely inane, unprovoked, childish outbursts of spite. God knows what made him do what he did.

One of the most venerable members of our club, Mr. Gaganov, had the harmless habit, when excited, of adding the phrase, "Ah, no, I won't let them lead me by the nose!" to every sentence he uttered. What harm is there in that? Well once, as he made this remark to a group of important visitors, Stavrogin, who had been standing in a corner and had taken no part in the conversation, walked up to Mr. Gaganov and, suddenly thrusting out his hand, caught the old gentleman's nose between his index finger and thumb and pulled him along a few steps behind him.

He couldn't possibly have had a grudge against Mr. Gaganov, so it must have been simply an unforgivable schoolboy prank. Later, people who said they had observed his face while he was pulling his victim behind him agreed that it was almost dreamy, "as though he'd lost his mind." But that was recalled only much later. In the heat of the action it was not the first but the second moment that struck them, by which time he must certainly have regained his senses. In any case, he didn't seem in the least embarrassed. On the contrary, he smiled maliciously and looked highly amused, "without," as they put it, "the least sign of regret for what he'd done."

There was a great commotion, and they all crowded around him. Stavrogin turned his head, looking into the faces of those nearest him without uttering a word in answer to their shouting. Then he again seemed to slip into his dream—at least according to the accounts of witnesses—frowned, walked determinedly toward the affronted Mr. Gaganov, and muttered very quickly, with unconcealed irritation:

"Of course—you'll have to excuse me . . . I don't know why I suddenly felt such a terrible desire to do a stupid thing like that. . . ."

The casualness of his apology was in itself a fresh insult. The din redoubled. Stavrogin shrugged and walked out.

It was all very stupid, to say nothing of its outrageousness. It was—one could see from the first glance—a deliberate and calculated insult to our entire society. And, indeed, everyone took it as such. To start with, Stavrogin was expelled from the club. Then they decided to present a petition signed by all the members of the club to the governor, requesting him (without waiting for the affair to be heard in court) "to restrain this notorious bully, this dueling fiend, from the capital by the administrative measures at your disposal, thus safeguarding the public peace of the town from similar scandalous breaches." And they added innocently, "perhaps some law could be found that would also apply to Nikolai Stavrogin." The purpose of this remark was to needle the governor about his relations with Mrs. Stavrogin. And they amplified it further with great zest.

As luck would have it, the governor was away. He had gone to a neighboring town to attend the christening of the child of a pretty widow whose husband had died during her pregnancy. However, he was expected back soon. In the meantime, the victim of the outrage, the venerable Mr. Gaganov, was feted and acclaimed: everyone shook his hand and hugged him, and the whole town called on him to assure him of their sympathy and admiration. They even planned to give a subscription dinner in his honor, but finally gave up the idea on his own insistence. Perhaps it dawned on them at last that the man, after all, had had his nose pulled and that that was hardly a suitable occasion for celebration.

And yet, how had it actually happened? How could it have happened? It is remarkable that no one in town ascribed this absurd act to insanity. This indicates that they expected such acts from a Stavrogin in full possession of his faculties. I myself don't understand it to this day, despite the event that soon followed it and seemed to explain everything and satisfy everyone. Let me say only that, four years later, Stavrogin frowned and gave the following answer to my carefully worded question as to what had happened that time in the club:

"I was not very well then, of course."

But I don't want to anticipate.

I was also rather curious about the general outburst of hatred against the "bully, the dueling fiend from the capital." They insisted upon finding in his action a deliberate intent to insult our entire community. The man had succeeded in antagonizing everyone. But what did they really have against him? Until that incident he'd never had a quarrel with anyone and had been as polite as a young gentleman in a fashion plate would be if a fashion plate could talk. I'd say it was his pride that brought all that hatred down on him. Even the ladies who'd begun by adoring him now loathed him more than the men did.

It was a great blow to Mrs. Stavrogin. Later, however, she told Mr. Verkhovensky that she had felt it coming every day and had even somehow expected "something just like that."

It is remarkable for a mother to admit a thing like that. "Here goes!" she had thought with a shudder. The day after the scandal in the club, she broached the subject very carefully to her son, trembling despite her determination. She hadn't slept all night. In the morning she had hurried over to Mr. Verkhovensky's place to talk things over with him and there had burst into tears, something she never did unless she was alone. Now she wanted her son to say something to her, to have enough consideration for her to offer some sort of explanation. Nikolai Stavrogin, who was always polite and considerate to his mother, listened to her for some time with a frown, then without saying a word, got up, kissed her hand, and went out of the room.

That evening—deliberately it seemed—he caused a second scandal that, although less violent and shocking than the first, was sufficient to whip up a general clamor because of the already prevailing mood.

Just after the scene between mother and son, Liputin arrived to invite Stavrogin to a party he was giving to celebrate his wife's birthday. Mrs. Stavrogin had long noted with horror her son's predilection for such vulgar company, but she didn't dare say anything. Besides, he had made other acquaintances among the third-rate members of our community and even lower. Such, apparently, were his inclinations.

Stavrogin had not yet been to Liputin's house, although he had met him socially. He guessed that Liputin's invitation was connected with the scandal he'd caused in the club, that being a local liberal, Liputin was delighted by it and thought sincerely that that was the proper way to handle venerable club members and that it was all to the good. He laughed and promised to go.

There were many guests at the party, and they were a lively lot if not particularly distinguished. Liputin, vain and envious man that he was, spared no expense when he invited people to his house, although he only did so a couple of times a year.

This time, his usual star guest, Mr. Verkhovensky, couldn't attend because of illness. There was tea, refreshment, and vodka. There were three card tables going and while waiting for supper, the young people danced to a piano. Stavrogin danced a couple of times with Mrs. Liputin—an extremely pretty little woman who was dreadfully intimidated by him—then sat next to her, talking to her and making her laugh. Suddenly, noticing how pretty she looked when she laughed, he put his arm around her waist and, in front of the assembled guests, kissed her on the lips, lengthily and with obvious relish, three times in a row. The poor, frightened lady fainted. Stavrogin took his hat, walked over to the nonplused husband, muttered with obvious embarrassment, "Don't be angry," and left the room. Liputin ran after him, personally got his coat for him, and with effusive politeness saw him off downstairs.

The following day there was an amusing sequel to this relatively harmless incident, a sequel that brought Liputin some credit and that he managed to exploit to full advantage.

At ten in the morning, Liputin's servant, Agafya, presented herself at Mrs. Stavrogin's house. This saucy, red-cheeked woman of about thirty said she had a message from her master for Mr. Stavrogin and that she absolutely had to give it "to the gentleman in person." Despite a bad headache, Stavrogin came out. His mother happened to be present during the delivery of the message.

"The master ordered me first of all to convey his respects to you, inquire after your health," Agafya rattled off cheerfully, "and ask how you slept after last night's party and how you feel about it today."

Stavrogin grinned.

"Please give my regards to your master, Agafya, and tell him from me that he's the most intelligent man in this town."

"And to that my master told me to tell you that he doesn't need you to tell him that and he wishes he could return the compliment."

"Really? But how did he know what I'd say to you?"

"I'm sure I don't know, but when I was already on my way here, the master came hurrying after me, without his hat, and said, 'And if, in despair, he tells you to say to me that I'm the most intelligent man in this town, don't forget to tell him that I know it myself and wish I could say the same of him. . . .'"

III

Finally the explanation with the governor took place. Our nice, kindly Ivan Osipovich had been presented with the club members' angry petition immediately on his return to town. He realized he had to do something, but couldn't decide what. The hospitable old man seemed rather afraid of his young relative. Finally, he decided to try to persuade him to apologize to the man he had offended and to the club membership as a whole, and to do so in a manner that would satisfy the offended parties—even in writing if they demanded it. The governor also thought he might find tactful arguments that would convince Stavrogin to leave us and go, for instance, on an educational trip to Italy, say, or some other foreign country.

Previously Stavrogin had wandered unrestrainedly all over the house, like one of the family, but this time the governor received him in a reception room. At a table in a corner, Alyosha Telyatnikov, a well-mannered clerk who was more or less a member of the governor's household, was opening postal packages. In the adjoining room, sitting by the window, there was a big, heavy colonel with whom the governor had once served in the same regiment. He was there on a visit. He was reading the newspaper, *The Voice,* and of course paid no attention to what was going on in the next room. In fact, his back was turned to it.

The governor approached the subject circumspectly. He spoke very quietly, almost in a whisper. But he got all mixed up. Stavrogin's attitude was quite unfriendly. There was nothing about it that suggested a warm family feeling. He was pale; he looked down and frowned as if he were trying to suppress an acute pain.

"I know you have a kind and noble heart, Nikolai," the old man said, among other things. "You're a well-educated man and you've been in contact with the upper crust of society. . . . Yes, and until this happened, even here your behavior was above all reproach, which was a great comfort to your mother, who is so dear to all of us. . . . And now everything has taken such a strange and dangerous turn! Let me tell you, as an old family friend, as an old relative sincerely concerned for you, whose words should never be taken the wrong way. . . . Tell me, what is it that prompts you to perform such wild deeds—deeds that are unacceptable by any standard of behavior? What is the meaning of these acts that appear to be performed by someone in a state of delirium?"

Stavrogin listened, irritated and impatient. Suddenly a sly, sarcastic expression flashed across his face.

"Well, I suppose I may as well tell you what prompts me to do these things," he said gruffly, and looking quickly around, he leaned toward the governor's ear. The tactful Alyosha

Telyatnikov had discreetly moved his table a couple of paces further away. In the next room, the colonel coughed as he read *The Voice*. Poor Ivan Osipovich hastily and trustfully thrust his ear closer to Stavrogin, for he was a terribly curious man. And at that point, something quite unthinkable—although in other respects quite understandable—happened.

The governor suddenly realized that, instead of whispering some interesting secret into his ear, Stavrogin had caught it between his teeth and was biting the upper part of it quite hard. The old man trembled all over, and his breath failed him.

"Nikolai, what sort of a joke is this?" he moaned in a distraught voice.

Alyosha and the colonel couldn't make out what was happening; to the end, it looked to them as if the two men were whispering secrets to each other. However, the wild, desperate look on the governor's face worried them. They kept exchanging questioning glances: should they rush to his rescue or wait a bit longer? Stavrogin must have noticed this and he clamped harder on the ear.

"Nikolai, Nikolai . . ." the victim moaned again. "All right, you've had your joke—that's enough now. . . ."

Another moment and the poor old fellow would probably have died of fear, but his tormentor relented and let his ear go. However, the state of shock continued for a full minute after that, and later the old man had some sort of an attack.

Within half an hour, Nikolai Stavrogin was arrested and taken temporarily to the guardroom, where he was locked in a special cell with a special sentry posted at the door. It was a drastic step to take, but the mild governor was so enraged that he decided to do it whatever the consequences, including Mrs. Stavrogin's ire. To everyone's amazement, when she hurriedly and angrily rushed over to the governor's to demand an explanation, Mrs. Stavrogin was refused admittance. She returned home without even having left her carriage and hardly able to believe it herself.

Then at last all their questions were answered. At two in the morning, the prisoner, who had been very quiet until then and had even slept for a while, suddenly started stamping and pounding on the door with his fists. He wrenched the iron grating from the window—a feat requiring unnatural strength —broke the glass, and cut his hands. When the officer of the guard arrived with his men and the keys and ordered the cell unlocked so his men could overpower and tie up the maniac,

Nikolai Stavrogin turned out to be suffering from an acute attack of brain fever. So he was transported home to his mama. Everything was immediately clear. Our three doctors expressed the opinion that the patient might have been delirious for the three previous days and, although he had appeared to be acting consciously and even cunningly, was by no means in possession of his senses—which, indeed, seemed to fit the facts. Liputin, then, had been the first to stumble on the truth. The governor, being a very sensitive and tactful man, was confused. But it is interesting to note that he too had considered Stavrogin capable of any mad action while in his normal state. The club members were also embarrassed at having missed such an obvious explanation. There were, of course, some skeptics, but none of them made much of an impression.

Stavrogin stayed in bed for over two months. A famous Moscow doctor was summoned for consultation. The whole town paid their respects to Mrs. Stavrogin, and she forgave them. Nikolai recovered completely and accepted without objection his mother's suggestion to take a trip to Italy. She also managed to convince him to make a round of farewell visits and, if he could bear it, apologize to those he had offended. He eagerly agreed. Word spread in the club that he and Mr. Gaganov had had a long conversation in the latter's home that had left the offended party fully satisfied.

Driving around on these visits, Stavrogin was grave and unsmiling. Although everyone seemed to receive him with great sympathy, they felt rather awkward with him and were relieved at the thought that he was leaving for Italy. The governor actually shed a tear, but for some reason didn't dare embrace him even at their farewell meeting. However, some among us apparently continued to believe that he was a good-for-nothing who was simply pulling everyone's leg and that his sickness had nothing to do with it. He dropped in on Liputin too.

"Tell me," Stavrogin said, "how did you guess what I'd say about your intelligence and so provide Agafya with a ready answer?"

"Why," Liputin laughed, "of course, I consider you an intelligent man too, so I could predict your reaction."

"Still, it was a marvelous coincidence. Now tell me, does that mean that, in sending Agafya to me, you regarded me as reasonable and not a madman?"

"Yes, as the most intelligent, the sanest man. But I did pretend to believe you were a bit out of your mind. . . . Anyway, you yourself guessed what I thought very well—you even sent me a sort of certificate of wit by Agafya."

"Well, you're not quite right there. I really wasn't too well then," Stavrogin muttered, frowning. "But wait—do you really imagine that I could go around attacking people while in full possession of my senses? Why would I do such things?"

Liputin looked puzzled; he didn't know what to say. Stavrogin had turned slightly pale, or at least Liputin thought he had.

"In any case, you have a very amusing way of thinking," Stavrogin added. "As to Agafya, I gathered that you'd sent her over to abuse me."

"Well, you didn't expect me to challenge you to a duel, did you?"

"Ah, that's right, I've heard something about your disliking duels. . . ."

"Why should we adopt French customs in our country?" Liputin said rather unhappily.

"So you're a stickler for our Russian national ways?"

Liputin looked even unhappier.

"But what's that? What do I see here?" Stavrogin exclaimed, pointing at a book by Considerant lying open on the table. "Are you a follower of Fourier by any chance? That wouldn't surprise me at all. But isn't this a translation from the French?" Stavrogin laughed, drumming on the book with his fingers.

"No, it's not a translation from the French!" Liputin said, with undisguised irritation. "It's a translation from a world-wide human language, not only from the French. It's from the language of the world-wide socialist republic of harmony, and not just from the French. You understand?"

"There isn't any such language, damn you," Stavrogin said, laughing.

Sometimes a mere trifle strikes people and sticks in their minds for a long time. We'll return to Stavrogin later. Meanwhile, let me point out that, of all the impressions our town had made on him, the most striking was that of the insignificant figure of this petty local government official; this envious, coarse family despot; this mean usurer who locked up the candle ends and the leftovers from dinner and at the same time fiercely advocated God knows what "social harmony"; who spent nights in rapturous admiration over visions of the fantastic future Utopia that he believed was about to descend upon Russia and our province as surely as he believed in his own existence. And he believed that this Utopia was about to

materialize in the very town where he had managed to accumulate enough funds to buy himself a house, where he had
married his second wife for her dowry, and where there was
not a man, including himself, within a hundred-mile radius
who in the least resembled a member of the future world-wide
harmonious socialist republic.

"God knows how such people get that way!" Stavrogin
thought wonderingly every time he remembered that surprising follower of Fourier.

IV

Our prince traveled for over three years, so that they almost
completely forgot about him in town. We heard from Mr.
Verkhovensky that he'd been all over Europe and also visited
Egypt and Jerusalem; that he'd later managed to attach himself
to some learned expedition to Iceland and actually to visit
that land. We were also told that he had spent a winter attending lectures in a German university. He only wrote to his
mother once every six months, sometimes even less often, but
she didn't seem to resent it. She humbly accepted her relations
with her son as they were, although she missed her Nikolai
and made up all sorts of daydreams about him. She never com-
plained or shared her dreams with anyone. She had even become somewhat distant with Mr. Verkhovensky. She seemed
to be making all sorts of secret plans, and grew stingier than
ever, saving money with even greater zeal and becoming more
and more irritated with Mr. Verkhovensky's losses at cards.

Finally, in April, she received a letter from Paris from her
childhood friend Praskovia Drozdov, the general's wife. They
hadn't seen each other or corresponded for over eight years,
but now, suddenly, Mrs. Drozdov wrote that Nikolai had prac-
tically become a member of their household, that he had become a very close friend of her only daughter, Liza, and that
he intended to accompany them to Verney-Montreux, in Switzerland that summer, despite the fact that in the family of
Count K. (a very influential personage from Petersburg) he
was also received like a son and had almost moved in on the
count in Paris. Mrs. Drozdov's letter was brief and its point
obvious, although she drew no conclusions from the above-
mentioned facts. It didn't take Mrs. Stavrogin very long to

decide what to do. Taking along her protégée, Dasha (Shatov's sister), she left for Paris by the middle of April and from there went to Switzerland. In July she was back by herself. She had left Dasha at the Drozdovs' who, she told us, were coming back to Russia by the end of August.

The Drozdovs also owned land in our part of the country, but General Drozdov (who was an old friend of Mrs. Stavrogin and a former army colleague of her husband) had found that his duties constantly prevented him from spending any time on his magnificent estate. Then, after the general's death, his disconsolate widow had gone abroad with her daughter and, while there, had decided to take a grape cure at Verney-Montreux during the second half of the summer. After that she intended to settle in our province permanently.

Mrs. Drozdov had a large town house that had stood empty and shuttered for many years. She was, in fact, a very wealthy woman. Like her childhood friend Varvara, Praskovia was the daughter of a rich government contractor and had received a big dowry when she married her first husband, Tishin. A retired cavalry captain, he was a gifted and intelligent man and very rich himself. When he died he left a substantial fortune to his daughter, Liza, who was then only seven. Now she was twenty-two, and a conservative estimate would have put her capital at two hundred thousand rubles—that is, without counting what would be left to her by her mother, who had no children by her second husband, Drozdov.

Varvara Stavrogin seemed very pleased with her trip. She felt she had reached a satisfactory agreement with her friend Praskovia Drozdov and as soon as she returned told Mr. Verkhovensky about it. Indeed, she chatted with him as she had not for a long time.

"Hurray!" Verkhovensky exclaimed, snapping his fingers.

He was very enthusiastic, especially since he had been feeling rather despondent during her absence. She had not even said good-by to him properly, nor had she confided any of her plans to "that old woman," fearing that his tongue would wag. She had been furious with him at the time because of a larger-than-usual gambling loss that he had just confessed to her. However, while still in Switzerland, she had felt she had been treating him roughly for some time. In fact, her sudden and mysterious departure had torn Mr. Verkhovensky's vulnerable heart, and to make things worse, he was suddenly beset with various other problems. First he was tormented by a financial difficulty of long standing that couldn't possibly be solved without Mrs. Stavrogin's intervention. Then, in May, our nice, meek Ivan Osipovich was replaced—and under rather unpleasant circumstances at that. And, while Mrs. Stavrogin was still away, the new governor, Andrei Antonovich von Lembke, took over. Immediately there was a noticeable change in everyone's attitude toward Mrs. Stavrogin and, naturally, toward Mr. Verkhovensky as well. At least he noticed some unpleasant and significant indications and was rather subdued by having to face everything alone. He knew from absolutely reliable sources that some of the ladies of our town intended to stop visiting Mrs. Stavrogin. The incumbent first lady, it was said, had a reputation for being very proud and haughty, but at least she was a real aristocrat, "unlike poor old Mrs. Stavrogin." Everyone seemed to have heard somehow that the new first lady and Mrs. Stavrogin had already met socially and had parted on decidedly unfriendly terms and that the mere mention of Mrs. von Lembke's name caused painful symptoms in Mrs. Stavrogin. But now, Mrs. Stavrogin's triumphant air and her scornful indifference to the ladies' opinions of her revived Mr. Verkhovensky's faltering spirits, and he immediately became gay and cheerful. He began to describe to her in gloating tones (in which she detected a certain obsequiousness toward herself) the arrival of the new governor in their town.

"I'm sure, *chère amie,* that you are already fully aware," he said in an affected voice, drawing out his vowels, "what a Russian administrator is like in general and, particularly, a newly promoted, newly baked we may say, Russian administrator. . . . But I don't suppose you'll grasp the meaning of what might be called 'administrative passion,' or what sort of animal it is."

"Administrative passion? No, I don't know what that is."

"Well . . . *vous savez, chez nous.* . . . *En un mot,* if you place some unspeakable nonentity anywhere, say in a wretched railroad-ticket office, the poor creature will start looking down on you as though he were Jupiter himself, as long as you want to buy a train ticket. Just *pour vous montrer son pouvoir.* And that's the type that attains to administrative passion. . . . *En un mot,* I read about some stupid sexton in one of our churches abroad—*mais c'est très curieux*—who kicked out of his church, and I mean literally turned out, a very nice English family—*des dames charmantes*—just before the beginning of the Lenten service—*vous savez ces chants et le livre de Job*—just because 'it ain't proper for them foreigners to wander around Russian churches except during proper visiting hours'. . . . The ladies almost fainted. . . . Well, that sexton was feeling his administrative passion to the full *et il a montré son pouvoir.* . . ."

"Make a short story of it if you can, my friend."

"Mr. von Lembke has left on a tour of the province now. *En un mot,* although he's a Russified German and Russian Orthodox, and even, to be fair, a handsome man, still in his forties—"

"How can you think he's handsome? He has bovine eyes."

"Yes, very much so, but I must concede to the opinion of our ladies—"

"Keep to the point, please. But, by the way, since when do you wear red ties?"

"That? . . . Just today—"

"And have you been exercising regularly? Do you go for a daily five-mile walk as the doctor ordered?"

"Not . . . not too regularly."

"I thought so! Even when I was in Switzerland, I knew you wouldn't do it," she said irritably. "From now on you'll walk not five miles but seven every day! It's incredible the way you've let yourself go—really unbelievable! You've not simply aged, you've grown quite senile in these past months. I was really struck by the sight of you when I first arrived, despite that red tie of yours. Ah, that tie, *quelle idée rouge!* And now tell me about von Lembke, if you really have something interesting to say. And please get it over with, for I'm very tired."

"*En un mot,* I was about to tell you that he is one of those men who've suddenly been entrusted with administrative power when they're in their forties, until which point they've been nonentities cooling their heels. Then, by finding themselves a brand-new wife or some other desperate measure . . . That is . . . he's out of town now . . . that is, I wanted to tell you that, they've been whispering things in his ear about me, that I'm a kind of perverter of youth, a provincial sower of the seeds of atheism. . . . And so he started making inquiries about me right away."

"Are you sure of what you're saying?"

"Yes, I've even taken some countermeasures. And when they went to him with talk about how you used to run the province, he dared to answer, 'Nothing of the sort will happen while I'm here.'"

"Is that what he said?"

"Yes—'Nothing of the sort will happen while I'm here.' And he said it with that arrogance of his. . . . And by the end of August we'll have the pleasure of seeing his wife. She's coming straight from Petersburg."

"No, from abroad. We met there."

"Vraiment?"

"In Paris *and* in Switzerland. She's related to the Drozdovs."

"She's related to them? What a wonderful coincidence! I've heard she's terribly ambitious and has very influential connections."

"Nonsense! Just very ordinary connections. She was a penniless old maid until she was forty-five. Then she hooked her von Lembke, and now, obviously, she's trying to push him ahead. They're schemers, both of them."

"They say she's two years older than he."

"Five years. Her mother wore out the seat of her skirts waiting to be received in my house in Moscow. She kept begging me to invite them to my receptions when the general was alive. And when she came, her daughter would sit all night with a great turquoise bow on her forehead, without ever being invited to dance. I'd feel sorry for her, and when two o'clock in the morning rolled around and she still didn't have a partner, I'd send her one. She was already twenty-five, but they dressed her in short dresses as though she were a little girl. It was positively awkward to invite them."

"I can see that bow now."

"I tell you, no sooner had I arrived than I stumbled upon an intrigue. You know—you've just read Praskovia Drozdov's letter—what could be clearer? And what did I find there? That fool Praskovia—she's always been a fool—looks at me questioningly as if to say 'What on earth have you come here for?' Can you imagine my surprise? I had a good look around and found that Lembke woman scheming away, and with her that nephew of old Drozdov—everything was clear! Oh, it took me no more than a blink of an eye to turn the tables on them and get Praskovia Drozdov back on my side. If they want to scheme, I'll show them what scheming is!"

"So you've succeeded in thwarting their plans. You're a real Bismarck!"

"I didn't have to be a Bismarck to detect falsehood and stupidity when I came across them. The Lembke woman is falsehood and the Drozdov woman stupidity. I don't think I've ever met a flabbier woman; she has swollen legs and, on top of that, a kind heart. What is more stupid than a kind-hearted fool?"

"A vicious fool, *ma bonne amie;* a vicious fool is even more stupid," Mr. Verkhovensky dissented bravely.

"Well, maybe you have a point there. I suppose you remember Liza?"

"Une charmante enfant!"

"Well, she's no longer an *enfant;* she's a woman, and a woman with plenty of character. She's high-spirited and quick-tempered, and I like the way she stands up to her silly, trusting mother. There was very nearly a real row about that nephew of old Drozdov's."

"Yes, but . . . he's really not related to Liza. . . . Unless he has views on her."

"You see, he's a young army officer and doesn't talk much—rather a modest young man, in fact. In all fairness, I must say that I don't think he ever approved of the whole intrigue. It was all the Lembke woman's idea. The nephew greatly admires Nikolai. So, of course, everything depends on Liza. Now, when I left, she was on the best terms with Nikolai, and he promised me he'd be back home in November. So it's the Lembke woman who's intriguing, and Praskovia is just blind. Can you imagine—she suddenly declared to me that all my suspicions were sheer fantasy! So I told her to her face that she was a fool. And I'm prepared to repeat it on the Day of Judgment. If it hadn't been for Nikolai's insistence that I leave things alone for the time being, I wouldn't have left without exposing that lying woman! She was trying to use Nikolai to get on the good side of Count K. She was actually trying to set the son against his mother! But Liza is on our side, and I've reached an agreement with Praskovia. Do you know, by the way, that the Lembke woman is related to Karmazinov?"

"What? Karmazinov is a relative of Mrs. von Lembke?"

"Certainly, a distant relation."

"You mean the novelist?"

"Well yes, the writer. What's the matter with you? What if he does regard himself as a great man? The swollen-headed creature! They will arrive here together; in the meantime, she's parading him around over there. I understand she intends to organize some kind of literary gatherings here, or something of the sort. He's coming here for a month to liquidate the last bit of some property he owned near here. I almost ran across him in Switzerland—without seeking it, believe me. However,

I hope that he'll be gracious enough to recognize me when we meet. In the old days he used to come to the house and write me letters. . . . Ah, I wish you dressed a bit better, Stepan—you get more slovenly every day. . . . Oh, the trouble you give me! What book are you reading now?"

"I—I—"

"I see—you're the same as ever: friends, drinking parties, the club, cards, and a reputation as an atheist. I don't like that reputation, Stepan. I don't like them referring to you as an atheist, especially not now. I didn't like it before either, because it was just empty chatter anyway. I suppose I was bound to say it finally."

"Mais, ma chère amie—"

"Listen to me now: as far as learning goes, of course, I'm nothing but an ignoramus compared to you. But when I was on my way back here from abroad, I kept thinking of you, and I came to one conclusion."

"What was that?"

"That we—you and I—really aren't the cleverest people on earth; that there are other people cleverer than we are."

"That's both witty and correct. There are people smarter than we, and they are therefore more likely to be right than we are. Therefore, we may have erred, right? *Mais, ma bonne amie*, let's assume I'm mistaken; don't I still have my eternal, supreme, human right to free thought? So, I have the right *not* to be a hypocrite and a bigot, even if it makes certain people hate me till they're blue in the face. *Et puis, comme on trouve toujours plus de moines que de raison* and since I fully go along with it—"

"What was that? What did you say?"

"I said *on trouve toujours plus de moines que de raison* and since I agree—"

"I'm sure you didn't make that up. You must have borrowed it somewhere."

"Blaise Pascal said it."

"I was sure it wasn't you. Why don't you ever say anything briefly and to the point yourself? You always drag everything out. I like his way of putting things much better than yours when you went on and on about administrative passion. . . ."

"Well, I must say I agree, my dear. But, in the first place, I'm no Pascal, and then, we Russians are incapable of saying anything in our native tongue. At least, we haven't said anything thus far."

"Hm . . . that may not be true at all. But you ought to write down and memorize phrases like that to use in conversation. . . . Ah, Stepan, to think that on my way here I longed to have a serious talk with you."

"Chère, chère amie!"

"Now, when all these Lembkes and Karmazinovs— Oh Lord, how far you've let yourself go! Ah, you make me so unhappy! I want those people to respect you, because they're not worth your little finger. But look at the way you behave! What can I show them? What will they see? Instead of standing like a living testament to our ideals and setting them an example, you surround yourself with all sorts of scum, acquire repulsive habits, and turn senile. You can't live without wine and cards; you read nothing but Paul de Kock's cheap French novels; you never write a word; and you waste all your time in idle chatter. Tell me, for instance, do you think becoming bosom pals with a disgusting creature like your Liputin is right?"

"Why do you call him *mine*? And why is he my *bosom pal*?" Mr. Verkhovensky protested meekly.

"Where is he now?" Mrs. Stavrogin asked sharply and sternly.

"He—he has the utmost respect for you. He's gone to Smolensk to receive a legacy left him by his mother."

"It looks to me as if all he does is receive money. And what about Shatov? Still the same?"

"Still bad-tempered and still a good man."

"I can't stand him. He's spiteful, and so full of himself."

"And how is Miss Shatov?"

"You mean Dasha? Why do you ask?" She looked at him with curiosity. "Well, she's fine. I left her with the Drozdovs. . . . And you know, when I was in Switzerland, I heard things about your son—bad things—"

"Ah, that's a stupid story. I wanted to tell you about it, my dear."

"All right, that'll do, Stepan; leave me in peace. I'm exhausted as it is. We'll have plenty of time to talk things over, especially the bad things. You splutter when you laugh, and that's really a sign of senility, you know! And how strangely you laugh these days. . . . Good God, what a lot of bad habits you've picked up! In your present condition, Karmazinov will never call on you, and that will make them happier than ever. You've finally revealed your true self for everyone to see. But that's enough, enough. Can't you occasionally show me some consideration at least and let me rest!"

Mr. Verkhovensky displayed his consideration for her and left. But he left greatly perturbed.

V

Mr. Verkhovensky really had picked up some bad habits, particularly lately. He had become noticeably more slovenly. He drank more and had become more tearful and nervous and rather hypersensitive to aesthetic values. His face had acquired a peculiar knack of changing instantly from, say, a solemn, inspired expression to a ridiculous and even idiotic one. He couldn't bear to be left alone for a moment and constantly craved distraction. He was always eager to hear any gossip and the latest local anecdotes. And if no one went to see him for a while, he walked disconsolately from room to room, stopped by a window, chewed his lips, and ended by almost whimpering. He had forebodings, fearing that something inevitable was going to strike him unexpectedly. He grew fearful and started to attach great weight to his dreams.

All that day and the evening that followed he was very despondent and agitated; he sent for me and talked to me at great length, but all rather incoherently. (Mrs. Stavrogin had known for a long time that he had no secrets from me.) I got the impression that something special was worrying him now—something that he couldn't quite formulate himself. Formerly, when we were alone and he began to tell me his troubles, a bottle had been brought in and things had soon looked brighter. This time there was no wine, and he appeared to suppress repeated impulses to send for it.

"And why is she so angry with me all the time?" he kept complaining like a little child. "All men of genius, all those who strive for progress in Russia have always been and always will be gamblers and drunkards who burn up their talents in alcohol . . . but I'm really not such a hopeless drunkard and gambler. Then she reproaches me for not writing. Strange idea! And why do I spend my days lying around? 'You,' she tells me, 'must stand like a monument of reproach!' But, *entre nous soit dit,* what's left for a man whose fate it is to 'stand as a monument of reproach' that's better than lying down? Doesn't she see that?"

I finally understood what was depressing him so much. That evening, he kept stopping by the mirror and looking into it. Once he turned his face from the mirror and said to me, "My dear fellow, I am a man who has let himself slip!" And indeed, until that very day, if there was one thing he had been sure of, amidst all those new ideas and views and Mrs. Stavrogin's changes of outlook, it was that he still possessed irresistible charms for her as a woman, not only because he was an exile and brilliant scholar but also because he was a handsome man. For twenty years he had harbored this flattering and reassuring conviction, and of all his convictions, it was probably the most painful for him to lose. Did he have a foreboding that night of the great trial he was to undergo soon afterward?

VI

Now I come to the rather amusing incident that marks the beginning of my story proper.

The Drozdovs came back at the very end of August. Their arrival, shortly before that of their relative, our new first lady, caused a great stir. But more of that later. For now I'll say only that Mrs. Drozdov, for whom Mrs. Stavrogin had so impatiently waited, brought unexpected trouble with her. Nikolai Stavrogin had left the Drozdovs as far back as July. He'd met Count K. and his family (including K.'s three daughters) on the Rhine and accompanied them to Petersburg.

"I could get nothing out of Liza," Mrs. Drozdov said. "You know how proud and stubborn she is. I could see for myself, though, that something had happened between her and Nikolai. I have no idea what caused it, but perhaps you can find out from Dasha. I think Liza was offended by something. And I must tell you, Varvara, I'm terribly glad to return your protégée. I'm not at all sorry to be rid of her."

This catty remark was uttered with a specially set face, and it was obvious that the "flabby" lady had prepared it in advance and was now relishing its effect. But Varvara Stavrogin was not a woman to be disconcerted by riddles and pinpricks. She sternly demanded more details. Mrs. Drozdov immediately changed her tone, and after a while burst into tears; she ended by protesting her deepest affection. This irritable but sentimental lady yearned for friendship just as Mr. Verkhovensky did, and her main complaint against her daughter Liza was that she was not a "real friend" to her.

Still, all Mrs. Stavrogin could gather for certain from the outpourings of friendship was that Liza and Nikolai had quarreled. But about the nature of the quarrel Mrs. Drozdov was obviously unable to enlighten her. As to her unpleasant remark about Dasha, the lady took it back, explaining that it had been made under the stress of irritation. But the main situation remained blurred and suspicious. According to Mrs. Drozdov, it had all started with "Liza's headstrong, sarcastic attitude," which "Nikolai, proud as he is—although very much in love with her—couldn't take, and returned in kind."

"And soon afterward," Praskovia Drozdov added, "we met a young man—a nephew of your Professor's, I believe. He had the same name. . . ."

Mrs. Drozdov could never remember the name Verkhovensky, so she always referred to Stepan as the Professor.

"Not his nephew, his son," Mrs. Stavrogin corrected her.

"All right, *son*; so much the better—what difference does it make? He's a young man like any other. He's very free and easy, but otherwise there's nothing special about him. Anyway, at that point, Liza did something she shouldn't have done: she started seeing a lot of that young man in order to make Nikolai jealous. I can't really blame her too much— it's a common feminine trick, and even rather charming, I think. But what do you suppose happened? Instead of being jealous, Nikolai became great friends with the young man himself, as though he either didn't see or didn't care. That made Liza furious. Well, then the young man left for somewhere or other (he seemed in a hurry, too), and Liza began to pick on Nikolai at every opportunity. She noticed that Nikolai spoke to Dasha sometimes; she threw genuine fits of rage that made my life impossible. I'm not supposed to get excited, you know—the doctors have warned me. And then I got so tired of that marvelous lake of theirs—besides, my teeth began to ache with rheumatism. . . . In fact, I've seen it in print—that the Lake of Geneva gives people toothaches; it's known for it. Then, on top of all that, Nikolai received a letter from the countess; he packed and left the same day. I must say they parted like good friends. Liza saw him off and was very gay and laughed a lot. But she was just pretending, I'm sure. As soon as he was gone, she grew quiet; she never mentioned him herself and never allowed me to. And I advise you too, Varvara, not to mention the subject in front of her—it would only make things worse. If you say nothing, she may want to talk about it, and you'll find out much more. I believe they'll make it up anyway if Nikolai comes back as he promised."

"I'll write to him immediately. If that's all there was, it was nothing. As for Dasha, I know her too well—it's all nonsense."

"I was wrong about Dasha, as I told you. They just talked—and not even in whispers. I was just so upset by everything. Anyway, Liza is as friendly with her as she was before."

That very day Mrs. Stavrogin wrote to her son Nikolai begging him to come back at least a month earlier than he had originally intended. But there was still much about the whole matter that she didn't understand. She turned it over in her head throughout the evening and during the night. Mrs. Drozdov's conclusions struck her as naïve and sentimental. "Praskovia was always sentimental even in boarding school," she reflected, "but a man like Nikolai isn't likely to fly from the sarcastic needling of a girl. There must be something more to it—if, indeed, there was any quarrel at all. There's that officer. . . . They've brought him along, and he lives in their house like one of the family. And why was she in such a hurry to take back her remarks about Dasha? I'm sure there is something she doesn't want me to know. . . ."

By morning Mrs. Stavrogin had a plan of action. It would solve at least one of the problems bothering her and was remarkable for its unexpectedness. I won't attempt to explain exactly what was in her mind when she conceived it, nor can I account for all its contradictory elements. I'll content myself with describing events just as they happened, and I decline all responsibility if they appear too incredible. I must, however, repeat that, by morning, she did not suspect Dasha of anything —if she ever had. She was much too sure of the girl. And then, she couldn't imagine her Nikolai falling for Dasha. In the morning, as Dasha was pouring tea, Mrs. Stavrogin studied her and muttered under her breath, "Nothing but nonsense!"

She noticed that Dasha looked tired, that she was even

quieter than usual and, in fact, rather listless. After breakfast, following a long-established habit, they sat down together to some needlework. Dasha was asked for a full account of her journey abroad, especially her impressions of the countryside, inhabitants, towns, customs, local arts, industries—indeed, everything she'd had time to notice. She was asked nothing about the Drozdovs or how she had got along with them. Dasha sat next to Mrs. Stavrogin, helped her with her embroidery, and answered everything in her rather weak, monotonous voice.

"Dasha!" Mrs. Stavrogin said suddenly. "Isn't there something special you'd like to tell me?"

Dasha stopped and glanced at Mrs. Stavrogin out of her pale eyes. "No, nothing," she replied.

"You're sure? You've nothing on your heart and conscience?"

"Nothing," Dasha said quietly, but there was a certain sullen determination in her tone.

"I was sure of it. I want you to know, Dasha, that I'll never have any misgivings about you. Now, sit tight and listen to what I have to say. Sit over there, on that chair. I want you to face me so I can see all of you. That's fine. Listen then: would you like to get married?"

Dasha gave her a long, questioning look, but she was not too surprised at the question.

"Wait. Don't answer. In the first place, there's a great difference in years, but I'm sure you realize how little that matters. You're a sensible girl, and you should be able to avoid the most glaring mistakes. And even so, he's still a handsome man. . . . Well, let me be direct with you—I have in mind Stepan Verkhovensky, for whom you've always shown so much respect. Well?"

Dasha's look became even more questioning, and this time there was surprise in it; she also blushed.

"Wait—say nothing; don't answer hurriedly! I've left you some money in my will, but still, think what'll happen to you, with or without money, if I die. They're certain to cheat you and take your money, and then you can say good-by to everything! But if you marry him, you'll be the wife of a famous man. Now, let's examine it from another angle: if I died tomorrow—although, of course, I've provided for him too— what would become of him? You see, I know I can fully rely upon you. Wait—let me finish. I'm fully aware that he's unreliable, ineffective, unfeeling, selfish, and afflicted with repulsive habits. But still, you ought to appreciate him because there are much worse men. You don't think I'd suggest some vicious brute just to get rid of you, do you? And the main reason why you should appreciate him is because I'm asking you to. Well, why do you sit there saying nothing?"

Dasha remained silent.

"Wait then—listen to me. He's nothing but an old woman, I know, but that's to your advantage, don't you see? He's a pathetic old woman, and there's certainly nothing about him to inspire love in a woman, except his helplessness. So try to love him for his helplessness. I'm sure you understand what I mean. You do understand, don't you?"

Dasha nodded.

"I never expected less from you. He'll love you because he has to—he must. He'll just have to adore you, Dasha!" Mrs. Stavrogin said in a strange, squeaky voice. "Anyway, knowing him, I have no doubt that he'll love you—and not only because he feels obliged. And remember, I'll be around. Don't worry, I'll always be around. He'll complain about you, spread all sorts of rumors, whisper nasty things about you to the first person he meets; he'll moan and whine unceasingly; he'll write letters to you from the next room—a couple of letters every day . . . but he won't be able to live without you, and that's what counts.

"You must make him obey you; if you can't, you're nothing but a fool. If he tells you he wants to hang himself, don't believe him—but keep your ear to the ground: anything may happen, and one day he may really end up hanging himself. His sort hang themselves not out of strength but out of weakness, so don't push him to the limit. That's the first rule in marriage. Remember, too, that he's a poet.

"Now listen to me, my girl, there's no greater happiness than self-sacrifice; besides, you'll render me a great service in this, and that's what's important. And don't think that what I've just said is a lot of rubbish. I know what I'm talking about. I'm looking after my interests; you look after yours, too. But I'm not forcing anything on you—it's whatever you say. Well, why do you sit there like that? Say something!"

"I don't really care, Mrs. Stavrogin. If there's no other way, I'll do it," Dasha said firmly.

"What do you mean 'no other way'? What are you trying to say?"

Mrs. Stavrogin glared at the girl. Dasha picked silently at the embroidery frame with her needle.

"You're a clever person, Dasha, but what you just said isn't very bright. It's true, of course, that I'm determined to marry you off, but it's not a question of there being 'no other way.' I've simply decided that it would be a good thing if you married and that the man should be none other than Mr. Verkhovensky. If he hadn't been here, I'd never have thought of marrying you off, although you're already twenty. . . . Well?"

"I'll do what you want, Mrs. Stavrogin."

"So, it's agreed, right? Wait—don't say anything—where are you going? I haven't finished yet. I'd left you fifteen thousand rubles in my will, but now you'll get them on your wedding day. Of that sum you'll give him eight—that is, not him but me, and I'll pay a debt he has for that amount. But I want him to know it's being paid with your money. So you'll have seven thousand left, and you must never give him a single ruble of it. Never. And never pay his debts, for if you do it once, there'll be no end to it. But, as I told you, I'll be around. You will receive a yearly allowance of twelve hundred rubles from me—fifteen hundred with all the extras—besides apartment and board, which I'll continue to supply as I have for him up to now. But you'll have to provide your own domestic help. As to the allowance, I'll pay you a lump sum once a year. You'll hold the purse strings, but I want you to be nice to him and let him receive his friends at home once a week. If they come more often, however, throw them out. But I'll see to that myself as long as I'm here. Now, if I die, your allowance will continue until his death—*his* death, do you hear?—because it is his allowance, not yours. As to you, besides the seven thousand—which you won't touch, if you're smart—I'll leave you another eight in my will. And that'll be all you'll get from me. I want to be sure that you realize that. Well, do you agree? Come, say something."

"But I've already answered."

"Remember, you're completely free. It will be just as you decide."

"Just tell me one thing, Mrs. Stavrogin. Has Mr. Verkhovensky said anything to you?"

"He has not. He knows nothing about it, but I promise you, he'll start talking soon enough!"

She got up very quickly, throwing her black shawl around her shoulders. Dasha blushed slightly and followed her movements with a perplexed look. Mrs. Stavrogin suddenly turned toward her, her face flushed with anger.

"You're a fool—a miserable little fool," she said, pouncing on Dasha like a hawk. "You're an ungrateful fool! Do you think that I would disgrace you? Do you? I tell you, he'll come crawling to you on his knees, feeling he's about to die of happiness! That's the way it will be arranged! You should know I wouldn't let anyone hurt you! Perhaps you think he'll marry you for the eight thousand—as if I were selling you. You're really an ungrateful little fool, just like the rest! All right now, get me my umbrella!"

And Mrs. Stavrogin hurried off on foot along the wet brick and plank sidewalks to Mr. Verkhovensky's place.

VII

Mrs. Stavrogin was telling the truth: she'd never have done anything to harm Dasha. Indeed, she felt she was being very generous toward the girl. Her indignation had been of the most noble and righteous nature when, as she wrapped herself in her shawl, she had caught Dasha's perplexed, distrustful gaze. She had sincerely liked Dasha ever since she was a child, and Mrs. Drozdov had been correct when she referred to the girl as Mrs. Stavrogin's "favorite." Mrs. Stavrogin had decided once and for all that Dasha was not at all like her brother, Ivan Shatov; that she was a quiet, gentle person capable of great sacrifices and very devoted to her, exceptionally modest, sensible, and above all, grateful. So far, Dasha seemed to have justified this estimation of her.

"There will be no mistakes in this child's life," Mrs. Stavrogin declared before Dasha was twelve. And with her propensity for clinging stubbornly to every plan, every fancy, every idea that attracted her, she immediately made up her mind to bring up Dasha like a daughter. She set aside a sum of money in the girl's name and engaged a governess for her, a Miss Criggs, who stayed with them until Dasha was sixteen. At that point she was abruptly dismissed for some unknown reason. After that, Dasha was educated by teachers from the town's secondary school who came to give her lessons at home. Among them was a real Frenchman who taught Dasha French, but he also, for some reason, was summarily dismissed. An elderly, impoverished, widowed gentlewoman also came in to give her piano lessons.

Dasha's principal educator, however, was Stepan Verkhovensky. In fact, he "discovered" her. He started teaching the quiet little girl before Mrs. Stavrogin even gave her a thought. And, as I said before, children became extraordinarily attached to him. Liza, Mrs. Drozdov's daughter, had also been his pupil between the ages of eight and eleven (of course, he taught her without remuneration—he'd never have accepted money from the Drozdovs). But in that instance, he had fallen in love with the charming child, and had created all kinds of romantic tales for her about the land, the history of mankind, and the organization of the world. His lectures about primitive men and tribes were as enthralling as the *Arabian Nights*. Liza, who listened ecstatically to his stories while he was telling them, later, at home, imitated him very amusingly. He found out about it and once surprised her during one of her performances. Terribly embarrassed, Liza threw herself into his arms and burst into tears. Mr. Verkhovensky also shed some exalted tears. But soon after that, Liza's family moved to another town, leaving only Dasha.

When the schoolteachers started coming to give Dasha lessons, Mr. Verkhovensky discontinued his studies with her and gradually stopped paying any attention to the child. This state of affairs prevailed for a long time. Then one day, when she was seventeen, Mr. Verkhovensky suddenly noticed how pretty Dasha had become. They were sitting at Mrs. Stavrogin's tea table. He spoke to her, was very favorably impressed by her answers, and immediately offered to give her a comprehensive course in Russian literature. Mrs. Stavrogin thought it was a wonderful idea and thanked him. Dasha was delighted. Mr. Verkhovensky began to prepare himself specially for these lessons, and finally they began. He started with the earliest period. The first lecture was fascinating. Mrs. Stavrogin also attended it. When Mr. Verkhovensky finished, he announced to his pupil that the next lecture would be devoted to *The Lay of Igor's Host*. Abruptly Mrs. Stavrogin got up and said that there would be no more lectures. He winced, but said nothing. Dasha flushed. And that was that.

And now, three years later, Mrs. Stavrogin had come up with her new idea.

Poor Mr. Verkhovensky, sitting all by himself, suspected

nothing. He felt rather sad and bored and kept glancing out of the window, hoping that one of his friends might turn up. But no one appeared. It was drizzling, and the air was growing raw; he thought they ought to have lighted a fire. He sighed. Suddenly he saw through the window a sight that startled him: Mrs. Stavrogin was coming his way. What could she want at this hour and in such weather? And why was she on foot and in such a hurry? He was so startled that he never thought of rushing for his coat and received her as he was, in his quilted pink smoking jacket.

"*Ma bonne amie!*" he exclaimed unconvincingly, moving forward to meet her.

"You're alone? Good! I can't stand your friends. Ugh! It's full of smoke in here. It really reeks! And look, it's past eleven, and you haven't even finished your breakfast! You enjoy living in such a mess, don't you? What are these scraps all over the floor? Nastasya, Nastasya!" she called out to the maid. "What's your Nastasya up to? Ah, there you are. Open those windows, my girl. And the doors too. I want them all opened wide; meanwhile, we'll go into the sitting room. I've come here on business, you know. And you, Nastasya, get busy. Sweep the room out properly for once!"

"The master always throws things all over the floor, ma'am," Nastasya whimpered shrilly.

"Then sweep up after him. Sweep fifteen times a day if you have to!"

They went into Mr. Verkhovensky's sitting room.

"What a poky sitting room you have," Mrs. Stavrogin said. "Now close the doors; I don't want her to hear. Ah, I must have this wallpaper changed. I'm sure I sent you the decorator with samples. Why haven't you chosen one? Sit down then and listen. Well—are you going to sit down or not? Where are you off to now? Where are you going?"

"I—I won't be a moment. . . ." Mr. Verkhovensky shouted back through the door. "Here—here I am."

"So you've changed your clothes." She looked him over, a sarcastic expression on her face. He had put his frock coat on over his pink smoking jacket. "Yes, that's certainly more fitting for what I have to tell you. Now, for heaven's sake, sit down!"

She gave it to him all at once, bluntly and convincingly. She hinted at the eight thousand rubles he needed so badly and mentioned the dowry. Mr. Verkhovensky's eyes nearly popped out. He started to tremble. He heard what she said, but it made no sense to him. He wanted to say something, but his voice failed him. He only knew that it would be as she had decided, that it was pointless to resist, and that for all practical purposes he was irrevocably married.

"*Mais, ma bonne amie,* it would be for the third time . . . and at my age . . . and she's only a child," he managed to say at last. "*Mais c'est une enfant!*"

"A child? She's twenty, remember. Will you kindly stop rolling your eyes? You're not on the stage. You're terribly clever and learned and all that, but you know nothing about life and you need a full-time nurse. If I die, what'll happen to you? She'll be a perfect nanny for you: she's modest, firm, and sensible. And, of course, I'll still be around for some time, for I hope I won't die this moment. She's a homebody and an angel of gentleness. This happy idea first occurred to me when I was in Switzerland. Don't you understand what it means, when I tell you myself that she's an angel of gentleness?" Mrs. Stavrogin suddenly shouted furiously. "You're living in a mess, and she'll introduce cleanliness and order here; everything will shine like a mirror. Do you really think that in presenting you with this treasure I should have to enumerate all the advantages you'll enjoy by accepting? Why, you should go down on your knees, you shallow, worthless creature!"

"But—I'm an old man."

"What's fifty-three? Fifty isn't the end of life; it's only half a life span. You're a handsome man—you know it very well. And you also know that she has great respect for you. If I died now, what would become of her? But married to you she'll be safe, and I'll feel reassured about her. You are a respected man; you have a name and a kind heart; you have an allowance that I consider it my duty to pay you. Perhaps you'll save her from all sorts of things; in any case, you'll be doing her an honor. You'll prepare her for life, mold her character, guide her views. So many young people are ruined nowadays because they're misguided! And in the meantime, your book will come out, and people will talk about you again."

"That's funny—I was thinking just recently of starting work on my *Tales from Spanish History,*" Mr. Verkhovensky said, gratified by Mrs. Stavrogin's adroit flattery.

"Well, there you are!"

"But—but what about her? Have you mentioned it to her?"

"Don't you worry about her. Anyway, that's none of your concern. Of course, you'll have to propose to her yourself—persuade her, beseech her, and all that sort of thing. But don't worry, I'll be around; I'll see that everything's all right. Besides, I know you're in love with her."

He felt dizzy; the room began to sway. He had a terrible thought that he couldn't push out of his mind.

"Excellente amie!" he gasped, trembling. "I could never . . . I never would have imagined you'd want to marry me off to another. . . ."

"You're not a young girl, Stepan. Only girls get 'married off,' remember that!" Mrs. Stavrogin said cuttingly.

"Well, maybe I didn't put it very well, but. . . ." He looked at her sheepishly.

"You certainly didn't!" she hissed at him scornfully. "Ah, good Lord, now he's going to faint! Nastasya, Nastasya! Get some water, quickly!"

But he didn't need the water. He recovered. Mrs. Stavrogin took her umbrella.

"I can see it's no use talking to you in your present state."

"Oui, oui, je suis incapable—"

"But by tomorrow you'll have had a rest and thought it over. Stay home, and if something happens, let me know—even if it's in the middle of the night. And don't bother to write me any letters—I won't read them. I'll come here tomorrow for a definite answer, and it'd better be a satisfactory one. Until then, try not to have any of your friends in; and I don't want to find this place in the disgusting mess in which it was this time. It's a real disgrace! Nastasya, come here!"

Needless to say, the next day he said yes. He couldn't help saying yes. There was a special circumstance that had to be taken into consideration. . . .

VIII

What we have referred to as Stepan Verkhovensky's estate—a fifty-soul affair by pre-Emancipation evaluation—didn't actually belong to him. The land (it adjoined Skvoreshniki) had been left by his first wife, and its rightful owner was their son,

Peter Stepanovich Verkhovensky. Stepan Verkhovensky had simply held the estate in trust for his heir, and when the son had come of age, he had given his father the power of attorney to go on running it. The arrangement was greatly to the young man's advantage: his father paid him an agreed sum of one thousand rubles a year while the actual income from the estate after the abolition of serfdom in 1861 was hardly half that. God knows how the figure had been arrived at; anyway, it was Mrs. Stavrogin who yearly made good on the thousand— Stepan Verkhovensky never actually contributed a single ruble. Indeed, he kept all the income from the estate for himself.

Furthermore, he drastically reduced its value by renting it out to some dealer and, without Mrs. Stavrogin's knowledge, selling for timber the woods that were its main asset. He sold the woods, bit by bit, for some time. The total value of the timber was at least eight thousand, but he got only five thousand for it. He went to such lengths because he lost heavily at cards in the club and didn't dare admit it to Mrs. Stavrogin. She almost gnashed her teeth with rage when she finally found out about it.

And now the son had announced that he was coming to sell his estate and had charged his father with carrying out the transaction. Because Mr. Verkhovensky senior had a generous and selfless nature, he felt guilty toward *ce cher enfant* (whom he'd last seen as a student in Petersburg). Originally the estate would have been worth thirteen to fourteen thousand, but now it probably wouldn't bring five. No doubt, from a strictly legal viewpoint, Mr. Verkhovensky could have invoked the power of attorney to justify his selling of the timber; he could also have claimed the right to deduct the difference between the annual one thousand rubles he had been sending his son and the actual income from the estate. But he was an honorable man, prone to noble gestures. He had conjured up a magnificent and dramatic scene and had decided to carry it through: when his Peter came, he would nobly lay out on the table the maximum sum possible—up to fifteen thousand, even—without saying a word about the money that he'd been sending the young man all the time. Then, shedding tears of affection, he'd press *ce cher fils* to his heart, closing all accounts between them.

Carefully and circumspectly he started to draw Mrs. Stavrogin into his dramatic plan. He even hinted that her participation would give their friendship and their ideals a specially

noble luster; that it would show how generous the fathers
of the past era were and, indeed, how noble their whole generation was compared with today's irresponsible young people
who were going in for socialism. He said many other things
besides.

Mrs. Stavrogin just let him talk. Then one day she announced that she was willing to pay the top price—that is,
six, maybe even seven thousand (four would have been quite
fair really, she said). She did not specifically mention the
depreciation amounting to eight thousand rubles caused by
the felling of the trees.

These talks took place about a month before the match-
making. Mr. Verkhovensky was very worried and preoccupied
about his son. At one time there had been some hope that
the young man wouldn't turn up at all—of course, the father
would have indignantly rejected use of the word "hope." Still,
strange rumors about young Verkhovensky kept reaching us.
After graduating from the university about six years before,
he had apparently just loafed around Petersburg. Then we
heard that he had been involved in the drafting of some
seditious proclamation and was about to be tried. Then he
turned up in Switzerland, in Geneva, and we feared he might
have fled abroad.

"He's a great surprise to me," the embarrassed Mr. Verkhovensky told us at the time. "Peter, *c'est une si pauvre tête!* He's
a kind, well-meaning boy, and awfully sensitive. I was so
pleased when I met him in Petersburg because he was so
different from the other young men of today. But *c'est un
pauvre sire tout de même.* . . . And, let me tell you, the whole
trouble stems from immaturity and sentimentality! It's not
the practical aspects of socialism that fascinate them but its
emotional appeal—its idealism—what we may call its mystical,
religious aspect—its romanticism . . . and, on top of that,
they just parrot others. But it puts me in a real fix: I have
many enemies, and *they* are bound to ascribe it all to paternal
influence. . . . Ah, my God, what times we live in! A boy like
Peter among the revolutionary leaders! . . ."

Soon afterward, however, Peter Verkhovensky sent his
father his exact address in Switzerland so his money could
be sent there. That proved he had left the country legally.
Now, having spent four years abroad, he was suddenly back
in Russia and had informed his father of his forthcoming
arrival in our town. That meant he had never really been in

trouble with the authorities. On the contrary, it appeared that someone in a high position had taken an interest in him. His letter had been mailed from southern Russia where he was on some important errand, trying to organize something.

That was an excellent piece of news, but where would the father get the missing seven or eight thousand rubles to make up a decent *top* price for the son's estate? And suppose there was a lot of arguing, shouting, and even a legal action instead of the noble scene? Mr. Verkhovensky had a feeling that his sensitive Peter wouldn't meekly stand for a financial loss.

"I feel it," the older Verkhovensky once confided to me in a whisper, "because I've noticed that all these desperate socialists and communists are incredibly stingy, avaricious, and terribly eager to own things. One might even say the more ardent a socialist a man is, the stronger is his need to accumulate goods. Why? Does it stem from the emotional element in their socialism?"

I don't know whether or not there was any truth in Mr. Verkhovensky's observation. I only know that Peter had been informed that his father had sold the timber from his estate and about the other operations, and that Mr. Verkhovensky was aware that he knew it. And I had read some of Peter's letters to his father. He wrote very seldom—less than once a year—but recently, in announcing his impending arrival, he had written two letters, one immediately after the other. In general, these letters were no more than brief notes; but since their meeting in Petersburg, father and son had adopted an informal tone toward one another, in line with the *modern* trend, and now Peter's letters sounded rather like the instructions that, in the old days, an absentee landowner sent to the serfs whom he had entrusted with the management of his estate.

And now, suddenly and miraculously, Mrs. Stavrogin had offered Mr. Verkhovensky eight thousand rubles, clearly implying, however, that she wouldn't let him have it unless . . . So there was no question about it—Mr. Verkhovensky had to accept.

As soon as she left, he sent for me and locked the door behind me. Of course, he had his little cry, talked a lot and beautifully, often losing the thread of his thought, made an accidental pun with which he was very pleased, and later had a slight stomach upset. In brief, everything was as usual. At one point he produced a picture of his pretty German wife who had been dead for twenty years and, staring at it, moaned a few times, "Oh, will you ever forgive me?" Indeed, he seemed a bit bewildered. We had a few drinks in this crisis, and he soon fell into a blissful sleep.

In the morning he dressed with the utmost care, constantly preened himself before the mirror, and tied his cravat beautifully. He discreetly sprinkled perfume on his handkerchief, but when he caught sight of Mrs. Stavrogin through the window, he quickly took another handkerchief, hiding the scented one under a cushion.

"Good!" Mrs. Stavrogin said when he announced his consent. "In the first place, it shows fine determination and, in the second, you seem to have heeded the voice of reason, something you seldom do when it comes to your private affairs. Still, there's no need to rush things," she added, looking at the elaborate knot of his white cravat. "Say nothing for the time being, and I'll keep quiet too. It's your birthday soon, and I'll bring her over for tea. But no drinks, remember. I think I'd better take care of it all myself. You'll invite your friends—but beforehand we'll decide together which ones we want to come. If necessary, you'll have to talk with her the day before. But at your party we'll make no formal announcement, just drop a hint unofficially. And, a couple of weeks later, we'll have a quiet wedding—as quiet as possible, in fact. It might even be best if you both went away for a while right after the ceremony—to Moscow perhaps. I might come along too . . . but, in the meantime and above all—keep your mouth shut."

He was surprised. He even protested feebly that he didn't see how he could go through with it without talking it over with the bride-to-be, but Mrs. Stavrogin replied sharply:

"And what would be the point of that? It may still fall through."

"What do you mean?" he muttered, completely at a loss.

"Just what I say. I still have to decide. . . . Oh, all right, everything will go off just as I said, after all. I'll break the news to her myself. There's no need for you to interfere: everything necessary will be said and done. How can you help matters? Well, you can't, so please stay away from her, and don't write her any letters either. Don't make a sound, and I'll keep quiet too."

She firmly refused to explain further and left looking rather upset. She may have been a bit surprised at his eagerness to comply.

Alas, he still didn't understand his real situation, and he hadn't yet considered the matter from other angles. On the contrary, he had a new, conceited intonation in his voice and was obviously pleased with himself.

"I don't like it at all!" he kept repeating, stopping in front of me and spreading out his arms. "You know what? I think she's trying to make things so difficult for me that I will finally refuse. She knows even my patience has limits and I too may be finally driven to say no! She tells me to keep my mouth shut and not to communicate with my bride-to-be! But why then do I have to marry at all? Just because she's got the ridiculous idea into her head? But I am a responsible man and may not wish to submit to the fancies of a cranky woman! I have responsibilities toward my son and toward myself! Doesn't she realize that I'm sacrificing myself? Perhaps I'm willing to go through with it only because I'm tired of life and nothing matters to me any more. But if she keeps irritating me like this, it *will* matter to me—I'll resent it and I'll refuse! *Et enfin, le ridicule*. . . . What will they say in the club? What will Liputin say? And she says 'it may still fall through.' . . . What do you think of that? It really tops everything! It's really too much to stand! No, really—I'm a man with his back to the wall!"

And all the time there was something whimsically conceited, something playful in those self-pitying complaints. Later we had a few more drinks.

chapter 3

'Another's Sins

I

A week later things became rather involved.

It was, by the way, a very hectic week for me, for, being his closest confidant, I never left my poor betrothed friend. He was oppressed by shame more than anything else, and since that week there was no one except me before whom he

could be ashamed, he was ashamed even before me. And
the more secrets he revealed to me, the more ashamed he
became and the more he resented me. In his morbidly
suspicious state, he imagined that everyone in town already
knew everything; he was afraid to appear in the club or
even to see the friends of his own circle. He even took to
going out for his daily exercise after nightfall, when it was
dark.

Another week went by, and he still didn't know whether
he was to be married or not. And he couldn't find out,
hard though he tried. He still hadn't seen the bride-to-be—
he wasn't even certain whether or not she was his bride-to-be.
Indeed, he wasn't certain whether there was a single element
of reality in the whole affair. And, for some reason, Mrs.
Stavrogin wouldn't even receive him herself. She answered
one of his early letters (and he wrote many more after it),
asking him plainly to please leave her alone for she was
very busy just then. She also informed him that she had
many important things to tell him and was waiting till she
had a free moment. He would just have to wait, and she
would let him know when he could come and see her. Finally,
she warned him that if he wrote to her again, she would
simply send his letters back unopened, because his writing
was nothing but a "silly, childish game." He showed me that
note, and I read it myself.

However, this vexation and uncertainty were nothing compared to his main concern. This constantly obsessed him,
causing him to grow thin and haggard. It was something of
which he was so ashamed he wouldn't mention it, not even
to me. Although he sent for me every day—he couldn't be
without me for two hours, for my presence had become as
indispensable to him as air or water—when I brought the
subject up myself, he lied to me and tried, like a small boy,
to divert my attention from it.

That rather offended me. Of course, since I knew him inside
out, I guessed his great secret from the start. At the time,
that secret rather discredited him in my eyes: I was still
young then and was most indignant at the coarseness and
ugliness of his suspicions. On the spur of the moment—perhaps I was getting rather bored with my role of confidant—
I was perhaps too severe in my judgment of him. In my cal-
lousness, I wanted him to make a clean breast of it all, although I realized that some things are hard to admit. On his

part, he saw through me too and realized how well I knew him and that I was furious with him. So then he was furious with me for being furious with him and seeing through him. My irritation could be called petty and silly, but it is very bad for real friends to be constantly together, face to face.

In a sense, he appraised certain aspects of his situation sensibly and was even rather subtle about certain points that he wasn't trying to hide.

"Don't imagine she has always been like that!" he'd say of Mrs. Stavrogin. "She was very different when we used to talk together. . . . Can you imagine—she could still keep up a conversation then! Would you believe me if I told you she once had some ideas of her own? Ah, she's quite changed now; she says that was nothing but old-fashioned chatter. She despises the past. Now she's always ill tempered and only concerned with her bookkeeping and accounting, and so unpleasant all the time. . . ."

"But why should she be unpleasant to you, since you're complying with her wishes?" I said.

"*Cher ami*," he replied, giving me a subtle look, "if I hadn't complied, she'd have been frightfully, frightfully . . . but less so than now that I have complied."

He was very pleased with the way he had put it, and we emptied a nice bottle of wine that evening. But that was just one bright moment; the next day he was gloomier and more miserable than ever.

I was particularly irritated because he didn't dare call on the Drozdovs, who had just returned from abroad, although they were eager to renew their old acquaintance and kept inviting him. He spoke of Liza with an enthusiasm that I couldn't quite understand. Of course, he had been very attached to her when she was a child, but apart from that, he somehow firmly believed that near her he'd find immediate relief from all his sufferings and would even resolve his major problem. He expected to find some extraordinary creature in Liza, yet he couldn't make himself go to see her, though he was on the verge of going every day. As for me, I was longing to meet her myself, and Mr. Verkhovensky was the only person who could introduce me. I often saw her, wearing an elegant riding habit, passing along the street on a beautiful horse accompanied by a handsome young officer, her late stepfather's nephew. I was immensely impressed by her. Although

my infatuation was ephemeral—I felt the hopelessness of
it soon enough—it is easy to imagine how impatient I was
with my old friend for his obstinate seclusion while it lasted.

First all our regular friends were warned that Mr. Verkhovensky was anxious to be left alone and couldn't receive
anyone for some time. He originally wanted to send everyone a circular letter to that effect, but I dissuaded him and
finally went to see each of them in turn and told them that
Mrs. Stavrogin had commissioned the old man—that was
the way we referred to him among ourselves—to put the
correspondence of many years in order and that he had
locked himself in to finish the job as soon as possible and
that I was helping him. Liputin was the only one I didn't
have time to see. I kept postponing my visit to him. As a
matter of fact, I dreaded it. I knew that he wouldn't believe
a single word of my story and that he would think there
was a secret being kept only from him. I was sure that, as
soon as I left him, he'd go tearing all over town prying and
gossiping. But, while I was still thinking about it, I ran into
him in the street. It turned out that he had already been
informed by others whom I had warned. Surprisingly enough,
he didn't inquire about Mr. Verkhovensky; instead, he in-
terrupted me while I was apologizing to him for not having
visited him and started talking about something very different.
True, he had plenty to tell me. He was very agitated and
was pleased to find someone to listen to him. He proceeded
to tell me all the local news: the arrival of the new governor's wife, who was "so full of talk about the new ideas";
the opposition to her that had already formed in the club; how
people were going around shouting about the new ideas and
how everyone had become caught up in them; and so on.
He talked without stopping for a good quarter of an hour
and he was so entertaining that I couldn't tear myself away.
I could never stand the man, but I must say he had a gift
for making people listen to him, particularly when he was
furious about something. In my opinion, he was a born
spy. He always knew what was going on in town, especially
if there was something scandalous about it, and it was surprising how nasty he could be about things that were obviously
none of his concern. I've always felt that the main trait in
his character was envy.

When later in the evening I reported my meeting with
Liputin and our conversation to Mr. Verkhovensky, he sud-

denly became very agitated and asked me an inane question:
"Does Liputin know?" I tried to explain to him that the man
couldn't possibly know anything because there was no one
who could have informed him. But Mr. Verkhovensky clung
stubbornly to his suspicion.

"Take my word for it," he concluded unexpectedly, "he
not only knows everything down to the minutest detail about
our situation, he knows things that neither you nor I know,
things that we may never find out about—or, if we do, it'll
be too late!"

I made no comment, but there was a lot behind those words.
After that Liputin's name didn't come up for five days.
I felt that Mr. Verkhovensky was displeased with himself for
baring his suspicions to me and saying too much.

II

One morning—it was seven or eight days after Mr. Verkhovensky had announced his willingness to marry—as I was
hurrying over, at eleven o'clock, to join my grieving friend,
I got involved in an adventure.

I met Karmazinov, "the great writer," as Liputin referred to
him. I had read his books when I was a boy. His novels and
short stories were very popular a generation ago and some
still are today. As for me, I drank them in; they were the joy
of my boyhood and youth. Later, my enthusiasm dampened
somewhat. I liked the novels with a special message that he
wrote later less than his early works, in which there was
much real poetry. As to his latest stories, I didn't like them
at all.

Generally speaking, if I must express my opinion on this
delicate matter, these mediocre talents who are taken for near
geniuses during their lifetimes vanish from people's minds as
soon as they're dead; even while they're still alive, they are
forgotten unbelievably quickly as soon as a new generation
replaces the one in whose time they were active. It is as though
the backdrop of a stage has been quickly changed. That certainly does not apply to the Pushkins, Gogols, Molières, Vol-
taires, nor to others who have something original to say.
Mediocre talents usually write themselves dry as they grow
older without even noticing it. And often a writer who has

been credited with profound ideas and is expected profoundly to affect society's thinking displays, after a while, such shallowness and poverty in his central theme that people are not really sorry he has written himself dry so soon. But these white-haired old men don't notice it themselves and they become very angry. Toward the end of their careers their vanity reaches really amazing proportions. God knows what they finally imagine themselves—gods at least, I'd say.

Karmazinov, it has been said, valued his connections with high society and the powerful of this world more than his own soul. He could, it was said, be terribly nice, disarming in his simplicity, and irresistibly charming—if he needed you for some reason or if you had been recommended to him in the proper places. But if by chance some prince, countess, or anybody who could harm him came by, he considered it his sacred duty to forget about your very existence, before you had even left the room, as though you were a fly or a chip of wood. And what's more, he sincerely considered this to be very good tone. Despite his excellent control of his temper and his perfect knowledge of correct manners, his vanity is said to have verged on hysteria. He was quite unable to hide his literary conceit even among people who were not particularly concerned with literature. If someone chanced to display indifference toward his writings, he became painfully offended and tried to avenge himself.

About a year ago I read an article of his in a magazine. Written in a very pretentious tone, it was supposed to be poetic and full of psychological insight. In it he described the sinking of a ship somewhere off the coast of England and how he had himself seen people being saved and dead bodies being pulled from the sea. The whole rather long, wordy piece had but one purpose: to tell us about the author. One could read between the lines: "See—that's how I behaved. You don't have to see that sea, those crags, those splinters from the breaking vessel for yourself—I've just described it all with my powerful pen. Why are you staring at that drowned woman clutching a dead baby in her dead arms? Look at me! I couldn't stand the sight, so I turned away from it. Here— look at me standing with my back to it. Now I'm trying to turn my head again, but in horror I close my eyes. Don't you think it's all frightfully fascinating?"

When I told Mr. Verkhovensky what I thought of Karmazinov's article, he agreed with me.

When it was rumored that Karmazinov was coming to our town, I was naturally anxious to see him and, if possible, to make his acquaintance. I knew Mr. Verkhovensky would introduce me, since the two men had been friends at one time. But then I bumped into him on a street corner. I recognized him because a few days before he had been pointed out to me as he drove past in a carriage with the governor's wife.

He was shortish and looked like a prim, little old man, although he wasn't actually more than fifty-five at the time. His face was rosy, and thick, graying locks of hair that had escaped from under his top hat curled around his small, neat ears. His clean little face could not be described as handsome: his lips were thin, long, and slyly pursed; his nose was rather thick; and his intelligent eyes were small and sharp. He was dressed in a rather old-fashioned style. His cloak might have been worn in Italy or Switzerland at that time of year. But at least all the minor items of his attire—cuff links, stiff collar, buttons, tortoise-shell lorgnette on a thin black ribbon, and signet ring—were highly fashionable. I'd have bet anything that in summer this man wore light shoes fastened on the side with mother-of-pearl buttons. When I ran into him, he had just stopped at the edge of the sidewalk and was looking carefully around before venturing across the street. Noticing that I was staring at him, he asked me in a melliflu-ous, although slightly shrill, tone:

"Would you please tell me how I can get to Bykov Street?"

"Bykov Street!" I exclaimed in great excitement. "Why, it's just over there, the second turn on the left."

"Thank you so much!"

Damn it! It had all been so sudden, and I was afraid I must have seemed obsequious to him. He noticed this immediately and in a flash knew everything about me—that is, that I knew who he was, had read all his books, had admired him since my childhood, that I felt very subdued before him and looked up to him with humility. He smiled at me once more, nodded, and walked off in the direction I had indicated to him. Now, I don't really know why I turned back to follow him, why I caught up with him and then walked abreast of him ten steps or so until he stopped dead.

"Perhaps you could now tell me where the nearest cab stand is?" he called out to me. I didn't like his tone or his voice this time.

"Cab stand? The cabs usually wait on Cathedral Square."

And now I nearly scurried off to get him a cab, which, I suspect, was just what he expected me to do. Of course, I immediately came to my senses and stopped, but he'd noticed all
right, for he was watching me with a nasty grin on his face.
And at that juncture something happened that I'll never forget.

He suddenly dropped a small brown leather bag he was
carrying in his left hand. Actually it was some sort of brief-
case rather than a bag, or rather something resembling an
old-fashioned lady's handbag. Anyway, whatever it was, I
was about to rush to pick it up.

I am absolutely certain that I didn't pick it up, but I did,
without a doubt, make the first movement. I couldn't possibly
conceal it, and turned beet-red like an idiot. Sly man that he
was, he immediately exploited the situation to his full
advantage.

"Please don't bother—let me . . ." he said radiantly when
he realized I wasn't really going to do it. He picked it up, as
if forestalling me and, nodding again, went on his way, leaving
me standing there like a fool. It couldn't have been worse if
I'd really picked it up. For about five minutes I felt that I had
been disgraced to the end of my days. But then, as I was
approaching Mr. Verkhovensky's house, I burst out laughing.
My meeting with the great man suddenly struck me as very
funny, and I was sure Mr. Verkhovensky would be amused
when I told him about it; indeed, I even thought I might act
it out for his benefit.

III

But to my great surprise I found him very different from
usual. True, he hurried forward to greet me eagerly and started
listening to my story, but he looked so lost that I doubted
whether he understood what I was talking about. However, as
soon as I pronounced Karmazinov's name, he flew into a rage.

"Don't mention him to me! I don't want to hear a word
about him!" he shouted, almost foaming at the mouth. "Here,
look! Go on, read it yourself!"

He pulled a drawer open and tossed onto the table three
sheets of paper scribbled over in pencil, all in Mrs. Stavrogin's
handwriting. The first note was two days old, the second was
dated from the previous day, and the third from that very

day. He had received it only an hour before I arrived. All three concerned a trivial matter involving the lady's vanity and Karmazinov. Mrs. Stavrogin was apparently worried that Karmazinov might forget to call on her. Here is the first note, dated from two days before (there may have been one from three days before and even from five—who knows?):

If he at last decides to visit you today, please don't say a word about me. Not a hint. Don't bring up any subject that may remind him of me.

V.S.

Here is the second note:

If he finally decides to call on you this morning, the most dignified thing, I believe, would be not receive him at all. I don't know about you, but that's the way I feel.

V.S.

And here is the last note, dated that very day:

I am sure there is a cartload of rubbish strewn around your room and that the tobacco smoke rises a mile high. I am sending Maria and Fomushka over; they'll clean up the mess in half an hour. Don't get in their way while they're working; go and sit in the kitchen. I am sending you a Bokhara rug and a couple of Chinese vases. I meant to give them to you a long time ago. I'm also giving you my Teniers (temporarily). The vases can be placed on the window sill and the Teniers should be hung under Goethe's portrait— it will be more conspicuous there, and that corner is always bright in the mornings. If he comes, receive him with great courtesy, but try to talk about superficial things or on some erudite subject—and your tone should suggest that you only parted yesterday. Not one word about me. Maybe I'll drop in to see you in the evening.

V.S.

P.S. If he doesn't show up today, he won't come at all.

I read the notes and was a little surprised that he should worry about such a trifling matter. I looked at him inquiringly and noticed that, while I had been busy reading, he had changed his usual white tie for a red one. His hat and walking stick lay on the table. He himself was very pale. His hands were trembling.

"I'm not interested in all her worries!" he yelled, beside himself, in answer to my mute question. "*Je m'en fiche*! She has the cheek to make all that fuss about Karmazinov, and yet she has no time to answer my letters! Here, see—there's a letter of mine she returned unopened yesterday, It's on the desk over there, under that book, *L'Homme Qui Rit*. And what do I care whether she's worried about her darling son or not? *Je m'en fiche et je proclame ma liberté*! *Au diable le Karmazinov, au diable la Lembke*! I've stored her vases in the entry hall, hidden the Teniers in the closet, and demanded that she receive me immediately. Yes, that's right: I said *demanded*! I sent Nastasya over with an unsealed note written in pencil just like hers. I'm waiting now. I want to hear Dasha's intentions from her own mouth, and let Heaven be my witness—or at least you. You will be my witness, won't you, my friend? I don't want to be ashamed of anything; I don't want to lie; I don't want any mysteries about this business. I want to be told everything—told openly, honestly, and frankly, and perhaps I will yet amaze this generation with the gesture I make! . . . Well, my good sir, would you call me a vile schemer now?" he said, glaring at me as though I'd actually said something of the sort about him.

I insisted he take a drink of water. I'd never seen him in such a state before. While he was talking, he kept tearing across the room from corner to corner. Then he suddenly stopped and faced me in an extraordinary attitude.

"Do you really think," he said, looking me up and down with great disdain, "that I, Stepan Verkhovensky, cannot muster enough moral vigor to pick up my pack—my beggar's pack—hoist it on my weak shoulders, and walk out of here forever the first moment my dignity and independence demand it? It wouldn't be the first time—despite the sarcastic little smile I believe you indulged in just now, my good fellow —that Stepan Verkhovensky has opposed noble determination to tyranny, even if it is the tyranny of an insane woman— the most degrading, the cruelest tyranny of all. You don't think I'll find the strength to go and end my life as a tutor to the children of some merchant or die of starvation in a ditch! Answer me! Answer me immediately! Do you believe me or not?"

But I preferred to say nothing. I even pretended that I didn't wish to offend him by saying no but still couldn't make myself say yes. Something in his explosion offended me—oh, not personally, no—but I'll explain that later.

He turned even paler.

"I seem to bore you, Mr. Govorov." (That's my name.) "Perhaps you'd rather stop coming here altogether," he said in that tone of smoldering, white fury that usually precedes a deafening explosion.

I jumped up in alarm. At that moment Nastasya walked in and handed Mr. Verkhovensky a note. He glanced at it and tossed it across to me. It contained only two words scribbled in pencil by Mrs. Stavrogin: "Stay home."

Mr. Verkhovensky grabbed his hat and stick without a word and walked out of the room. I followed him mechanically. Suddenly voices and hurried footsteps resounded in the passage. He stopped as if struck by lightning.

"It's Liputin. . . . I'm lost!" he whispered, seizing me by the hand.

Just then, Liputin walked into the room.

IV

Why Liputin's arrival should signify his perdition, I had no idea and, in any case, I didn't attach any great importance to his words: I felt they were due to his shattered nerves.

Liputin's sudden appearance, however, suggested that he had gained the special privilege of entering this house whether visitors were welcome or not. Noticing the petrified Mr. Verkhovensky's blank stare, he immediately cried out:

"I have a visitor with me—a very special one—so I've taken the liberty of intruding upon you! Meet Alexei Kirilov, a brilliant construction engineer. And what's more, he knows your dear son Peter well and has a message from him for you. He's just arrived."

"The message—he's making that up," the newcomer said rudely. "Never was a message. But it's true I know Verkhovensky, and I even saw him near Kharkov just ten days ago."

Mr. Verkhovensky shook hands with them mechanically and motioned them to sit down. Thereupon he glanced at me, then at Liputin, and as if he had suddenly recovered his senses, hurriedly sat down too, without realizing he was still holding his hat and walking stick in his hand.

"I see," Liputin said, "that you were about to go out yourself, although I was told that you'd fallen ill with all that work."

"Yes, I'm ill . . . I thought a bit of fresh air would do me good," Mr. Verkhovensky said, tossing his hat and walking stick on the sofa and blushing.

In the meantime, I studied the visitor. He was quite young, twenty-seven or so, decently dressed, spare and wiry. He had dark hair, a pale, somewhat unwashed-looking complexion, and black lusterless eyes. He seemed dreamy and absent-minded and spoke abruptly and rather ungrammatically, arranging his words in peculiar sequences and getting mixed up when he had to cope with long sentences.

Liputin had noticed what a fright he'd caused Mr. Verkhovensky and was very pleased about it. He installed himself in a wicker chair that he pulled out into the middle of the room to be equidistant from Mr. Verkhovensky and the engineer, who were sitting on sofas at opposite sides of the room.

"I haven't seen Peter for a long time. . . . You met abroad, I suppose?" Mr. Verkhovensky muttered awkwardly.

"I knew him here and abroad."

"Mr. Kirilov has just returned home after four years' absence," Liputin chimed in. "He went abroad to specialize further in his profession, and he hopes to get a post here on the construction of the railroad bridge. He's waiting for an answer to his application now. He was introduced to Mrs. Drozdov and her daughter Elizaveta by the young Mr. Verkhovensky."

The engineer sat stiffly, listening with awkward impatience. He seemed to be furious about something.

"He knows Nikolai Stavrogin too," Liputin added.

"So you know Mr. Stavrogin," Mr. Verkhovensky said.

"I know that one too."

"I—I haven't seen my son Peter for a very long time . . . and I hardly feel entitled to call myself his father . . . yes, just as I said. Tell me, how was he? Why did he stay behind after you left?"

"Well, I just drove on, and that's all there is to it. . . . He'll manage to get here by himself." Kirilov again answered abruptly. He seemed really angry.

"So he's coming here! At last! You see—I haven't seen him for much too long a time. It has been too long. . . ."

Mr. Verkhovensky seemed to have become bogged down. "So now I'm waiting for my dear boy before whom I feel so guilty! What I mean to say is that, leaving him, in Petersburg, I . . . well, to cut the story short, I didn't think much of him, *quelque chose dans ce genre*. As a boy, you know, he was very sensitive and very . . . fearful. When he went to bed he said his prayers on his knees and made the sign of the cross over his pillow. He believed he might die during the night if he didn't. . . . *Je m'en souviens. Enfin*, he didn't have any aesthetic sense—no feeling for higher things, for anything universal—no germ of any great idea for the future . . . *c'etait comme un petit idiot*. But I think I'm getting all mixed up. Forgive me . . . you've found me in a state. . . ."

"Are you serious about him crossing his pillow?" the engineer asked with sudden interest.

"Yes, he did make the sign of the cross over his pillow."

"Just curious. Go on."

Mr. Verkhovensky looked questioningly at Liputin.

"I'm very grateful to you for coming to see me, but I must confess that, at this moment, I cannot. . . . May I ask you, however, where you're staying?"

"Filipov's house, on Nativity Street."

"That's the house where Shatov lives," I said unthinkingly.

"Yes, the very same house," Liputin cried cheerfully, "but Shatov lives upstairs in the attic, and Mr. Kirilov is staying in Captain Lebyatkin's apartment downstairs. But he knows Shatov and his wife—he saw a lot of them when they were abroad."

"Really? Do you know something about the hapless marriage *de ce pauvre ami* or about that woman?" Mr. Verkhovensky seemed carried away. "You're the first man I've ever met who knows her personally, and if—"

"Bunk!" Kirilov said, flushing heavily. "You really distort everything, Liputin. I never saw a lot of Shatov's wife. In fact, I only saw her once. Not too close, either. Why are you making all this up, Liputin?"

He turned sharply on the sofa and grabbed his hat, then tossed it away, settled down once again, and fixed his black eyes challengingly on Mr. Verkhovensky. I couldn't make out what it was that irritated him so much.

"I beg your pardon," Mr. Verkhovensky said solemnly. "I realize it's a delicate matter—"

"Nothing delicate about it—it's just a shameful mess. And

when I said 'bunk!' it wasn't addressed to you but to Liputin because he keeps adding things. I'm sorry if you took it as addressed to you. I know Shatov, but I don't know his wife. I know nothing about her!"

"I gathered that, and if I insisted, it was only because I am so fond of our poor friend, *notre irascible ami,* and have always taken a great interest in him. I feel he's changed his former opinions—which were perhaps immature, but nevertheless correct—a bit too radically. And the way he goes around shouting about Holy Mother Russia now—*notre sainte Russie*—I can only explain such an organic reversal—I must call it that—by some violent upheaval in his personal life, namely his unhappy marriage. I, who have studied my poor, dear Russia and know it like the back of my hand—I, who have devoted my life to the service of the Russian people, assure you that he knows nothing about the Russian masses. Furthermore—"

"Now, I—I know nothing about the Russian people or the masses, and I have no time to study them," Kirilov cut in impatiently and again twisted noisily on his sofa. Mr. Verkhovensky stopped in the middle of his sentence, gaping.

"But he does, he does study them!" Liputin interposed. "Mr. Kirilov is right now doing some interesting research on the causes of the increasing incidence of suicides in Russia and, in general, on the causes of an increase or decrease of suicides in a society. He has come, I understand, to remarkable conclusions."

Kirilov looked terribly agitated and muttered angrily,

"You have no right. . . . It's not really research. I won't bother with nonsense. I asked you confidentially just on the off-chance. It's not a study for publication, and you have no right . . ."

"Sorry. So I'm wrong to refer to your literary effort as research. Mr. Kirilov simply collects observations; he does not touch upon the essence of the matter or, as we might say, the moral aspect of it. Indeed, he denies there is any such thing as morality and he advocates the latest principle—total destruction in the name of the ultimate good. Mr. Kirilov has already demanded that more than one hundred million heads roll so that reason may be introduced in Europe, and that considerably exceeds the figure proposed at the last peace congress. In that sense, Alexei Kirilov is ahead of everyone."

Kirilov listened with a faintly scornful smile. After Liputin's comment, there was silence for about half a minute.

"What you just said, Liputin, is stupid," Kirilov said, finally, with a certain dignity. "You picked up the few points I happened to develop in front of you and twisted them to suit yourself. But you have no right, because I never talk about those things. I despise a lot of talk. If I find convincing reasons, it's enough. . . . You've acted stupidly. I'm not trying to reason about those points—they've been settled. I hate reasoning. I never want to reason. . . ."

"And perhaps that's very sensible of you," Mr. Verkhovensky couldn't resist adding.

"I apologize to you. I'm not quarreling with anyone present here," Kirilov muttered excitedly. "For four years I've seen very few people. For four years I've spoken very little and avoided everyone because of a certain purpose I had that is no one's business. Now Liputin has found out about it and it amuses him. I can see that, but I don't care. I am not offended. I'm just annoyed at the liberties he takes. . . . Now, if I don't explain myself, I don't want you to think it's because I'm afraid you may report me to the authorities. No, please—don't think that; you see, it's bunk in that sense."

No one had an answer to these words. We all simply exchanged glances. Even Liputin forgot to snigger.

"Gentlemen, I'm awfully sorry," Mr. Verkhovensky said, rising determinedly from the sofa, "but I am unwell and rather upset. You'll have to excuse me."

"Ah, you want us to go," Kirilov said, snatching up his cap. "I'm glad you reminded us, I'm very forgetful." He got up and, with a good-humored expression, walked over to Mr. Verkhovensky with outstretched hand. "I'm sorry you don't feel well and that I came."

"I wish you every success now that you have returned," Mr. Verkhovensky said, shaking his hand warmly and unhurriedly. "I understand from what you've told us that you've had to stay abroad for four years, avoiding people for your own reasons, and so you've forgotten Russia. You must look upon us stay-at-home Russians—just as we are bound to look upon you—with a certain surprise. *Mais cela passera.* There's only one point that remains unclear to me: you wish to build that railroad bridge for us, but at the same time you proclaim the principle of total destruction. They won't let you build any bridge."